#8 Camp Clodhopper

Look for these other books
in the Bad News Ballet series:

Bad News Ballet

#8 Camp Clodhopper

Jahnna N. Malcolm

AN
APPLE
PAPERBACK

SCHOLASTIC INC.
New York Toronto London Auckland Sydney

ISBN 0-590-43396-2

Copyright © 1990 by Jahnna Beecham and Malcolm Hillgartner. All rights reserved. Published by Scholastic Inc. APPLE PAPERBACKS is a registered trademark of Scholastic Inc.

12 11 10 9 8 7 6 5 4 3 2 1   0 1 2 3 4 5/9

Printed in the U.S.A.   40

First Scholastic Printing, August 1990

For Rob Proctor,
who makes me laugh

Chapter One

"School's out, school's out,
teacher's let the mules out;
One went east, and one went west,
and one went to camp,
and that was the best!"

Five girls sang at the top of their lungs as they rolled along the Ohio road, heading for summer camp. Mary Bubnik sat in the front seat of her mother's old green Volvo, singing the loudest. Her tight blonde curls jiggled and bounced with each word she sang.

"Oh, y'all, I am *soooooo* excited!" Mary drawled in her southern accent. "A lot of kids at my school are just going to regular old camp, but not us. *We*

1

get to go to the Claude Harper Camp for the Performing Arts."

The five friends had decided they needed to take ballet lessons during the summer to insure that they would be promoted to the more advanced class at the Deerfield Academy of Dance in the fall. But no one wanted to give up their vacation. The performing arts camp was the perfect solution for combining lessons and fun.

"Just imagine," Zan Reed said breathlessly. "There'll be poetry readings in the lodge, wonderful stories told around the campfire, and classical music played live all day long." The thin black girl leaned her head back against the torn leather cover of the backseat and sighed with content.

"I just know we're going to meet a whole bunch of new and interesting people," Mary Bubnik added.

Gwendolyn Hays was sitting behind the driver's seat, with her back against the window. "I'm glad we don't have to do any of that awful campy stuff," she said, "like hiking, and canoeing, and rubbing logs together." The plump redhead squinched up her nose in distaste.

Kathryn McGee, who was wedged between Gwen and Zan, flipped up the visor of her baseball cap. "Rubbing logs together?" she asked. "Why would you do that?"

"To start campfires." Gwen blinked at McGee matter-of-factly behind her wire-rimmed glasses. "We had to do that when I was a Bluebird and, believe me, it was no fun. In fact, our leader couldn't even get the fire started. And it was cold out, and we were starved."

"What did you do?" Mary Bubnik asked.

"The only thing we could do. Rent a motel room and eat out at McDonald's."

McGee dug in the pocket of her sweatshirt jacket and pulled out the faded color brochure she had received in the mail. She pored over it for the hundredth time. "What I like is we can take ballet lessons but we don't have to be in a stuffy old studio. We'll be — " She read from the brochure in a loud clear voice: " 'Dancing under the whispering pines that encircle Lake Charles. The Claude Harper Camp for the Performing Arts promises to turn young dancers into accomplished ballerinas.' "

"Accomplished ballerinas?" Gwen arched a worried eyebrow. "That sounds like hard work." She struggled to turn sideways and glanced at the brochure over McGee's shoulder. "I thought this was supposed to be fun."

"Don't worry, it will be," Mary Bubnik said, her blue eyes twinkling with anticipation. "Camps are always fun."

"I wouldn't bet on it," Rocky Garcia grumbled from the other side of the backseat. She sat with her head pressed mournfully against the window, her wild black hair mushrooming about her face. Rocky wasn't looking forward to camp for one reason, and one reason only. She couldn't swim. None of the others knew that and Rocky wasn't about to let them know — now, or ever.

McGee leaned forward and showed Rocky the picture on the back of the brochure. "Look, Rocky, we won't always be dancing. It says here that we can go horseback riding with a real wrangler." McGee grinned happily. "I *love* horses!"

"That sounds terrible," Gwen groaned. "Sweaty horses, and those terrible horseflies. Have you ever seen one of them? They're huge! And, boy, do they hurt when they bite you."

"Well, you don't have to go," McGee retorted, flipping one chestnut braid over her shoulder. "Horseback riding is optional."

"So are canoeing and hiking," Gwen said, pointing to the picture in the brochure. "And that's just fine with me." She shuddered. "There's no telling how many different kinds of bugs you'll meet in the wilderness."

Zan laughed. "So what you're saying is, you truly don't like bugs."

Gwen nodded firmly. "Of any kind." She confidently patted the pink dance bag that usually held her ballet shoes and supply of snacks. "Luckily I came prepared." Gwen unzipped the top and read off the labels on the different cans and bottles that clinked together inside. "Buzz Off, No-Bite, Bug Zap, and Off Limits."

"Why do you have so many?" Mary Bubnik asked. "Don't they all do the same thing?"

Gwen shook her head. "One's a lotion, another's a spray, one's for nighttime, and this one is to squirt around your cabin. And just in case those don't work..." She felt around to the side pocket of her dance bag. "I brought mosquito netting."

"Let me see that brochure," Rocky said, reaching across Zan. She unfolded the shiny pamphlet and lay it flat across her lap.

The first picture was a glorious panorama of a deep blue lake surrounded by tall pines. Inside there were smaller pictures of kids playing cellos and violins along the water's edge. They were dressed in striped bell-bottom jeans with big white belts and ribbed tee shirts. Another shot showed four girls in leotards posed on the dock. Each dancer wore thick eyeliner and pale white lipstick.

"These pictures look really old," Rocky observed.

Zan peered over Rocky's shoulder. "That's true. Look at their hairdos. They look like photographs from my parents' high school yearbook in the sixties."

McGee shrugged. "Maybe they figured they didn't need to take new pictures. I mean, after all, a tree's a tree. And ballet dancers always wear leotards."

"Yeah," Gwen chimed in. "They've probably fixed up the camp a lot since then. You know, added a hot tub and a giant-screen TV. All that kind of stuff."

Mrs. Bubnik flicked on her turn signal and as she rounded the corner by a thick clump of trees, Lake Charles sparkled off in the distance.

"Look, you guys!" Mary Bubnik squealed from the front seat. She leaned forward and peered through the windshield. "I think I see our camp."

"Where?" The four girls crammed together in the backseat all leaned forward at once. Big stone gates loomed off to their right. As the car came closer, the girls could see a huge timbered lodge up on the hill, surrounded by charming rustic cabins.

"They have red clay tennis courts," Zan gasped.

"Look at the pool," McGee shouted. "It's hum*on*gus!"

Mrs. Bubnik slowed the car to almost a crawl so the girls could get a better look. The sight of the huge Olympic-size swimming pool gleaming in the sun made Rocky groan out loud. Beside the pool was a broad manicured lawn, where the gang could see several girls in white shorts and tops playing croquet.

"Look at the wonderful uniforms they give you," Zan cried.

"Look at the snack shack." Gwen pointed to a small wooden shed with a cheery striped awning and four red stools. More girls in crisp white outfits lounged against the counter, sipping drinks and chatting.

"Geez Louise!" McGee exclaimed, clapping her hands together. "This camp is fabulous!"

Mrs. Bubnik checked the name on the tiny brass plate on the gate with the address she had written on the back of an envelope. "Sorry, girls," she declared. "This isn't your camp. This is Camp Scotsvale."

"Oh."

Five disappointed girls fell back against their seats as Mrs. Bubnik continued along the narrow paved road circling the lake. It soon turned into a dusty gravel road.

"Roll up your windows!" Mrs. Bubnik shouted as clouds of dust billowed up around the car. They all started coughing and choking.

Gwen tapped Mrs. Bubnik on the shoulder. "Are you sure this is the right way? This road looks deserted."

Mrs. Bubnik checked her directions again and said, "According to the instructions they gave me over the phone, we should be just about there."

As she spoke she drove past a wooden sign that had once hung on little chains between two posts. One of the chains was broken so the right side of the sign dangled on the ground.

"Back up!" Rocky shouted. "I think we just passed it."

Mrs. Bubnik put the car in reverse and backed up to the posts. Mary Bubnik rolled down her window and squinted at the faded sign. "This is it, all right." She pointed to a winding dirt road that curved off to the right. "Follow that road, but be careful of the rocks, Mom."

A loud clunk reverberated under the car as the

7

green Volvo scraped over a large boulder stuck in the middle of the road.

"They must have forgotten to fix the sign," Mary Bubnik said, trying to sound cheerful. "I'm sure the camp will be just great."

No one responded. They were all staring glumly at the large metal Quonset hut that loomed up out of the dust. An ancient basset hound was lounging in the sun on the small porch.

"That looks like one of those buildings the Air Force uses for temporary offices," Rocky said, leaning forward. Her dad was a sergeant in the Air Force and she'd spent her entire life on military bases.

"Those can't be *our* cabins," Gwen gasped. Off to one side of the Quonset hut sat drab yellow tents on wooden platforms. She spun frantically in her seat looking for trim little cabins like the ones they'd seen at the last camp.

"I'm afraid they are," Zan said miserably. She had had visions of strolling through groves of mossy woods, writing poetry in her journal. But this dusty campground looked like an old trailer park.

"It looks like we'll be roughing it," Mary Bubnik murmured.

"What do you mean, *we?*" Gwen crossed her arms stubbornly. "I'm not sleeping in those. No way."

Only Rocky was smiling; there wasn't a swimming

pool in sight. She reached across and jokingly nudged McGee. "Yo, McGee. Check out the stables."

"Where?" McGee's face lit up for a moment, but quickly fell as they passed a rusty blue pick-up truck. A fat old horse was tied to the fender, lazily eating the few tufts of grass surrounding the car. McGee stuck her tongue out at Rocky. "Very funny."

As Mrs. Bubnik pulled up to the main building, Mary Bubnik murmured, "Where are all the people in neat outfits, playing music and croquet? It looks like we're the only ones here."

At that moment, the screen door to the big metal building banged open and out stepped a square muscular woman in shorts. She wore a visor over her cropped dyed-blonde hair and a big metal whistle hung from a cord around her neck. She spotted the car full of girls and immediately snapped to attention with her hands on her hips.

"Welcome, campers!" the woman bellowed in an unbelievably loud voice. "I'm Sergeant Margaret Ledbetter, formerly of the U.S. Marine Corps. But you can call me Sarge." Her lips parted in what was supposed to be a grin. "I'm your counselor in charge of physical fitness."

"Physical fitness," Gwen repeated in horror. "The brochure didn't say anything about that."

"Mrs. Bubnik," McGee and Rocky pleaded together. "Turn the car around. Let's get out of here before it's — "

9

"Too late," Gwen groaned, as Marge Ledbetter threw open the back door of the car.

"Grab your gear, girls, and I'll show you your quarters. You are Birch Patrol."

They stared at the woman in shock, unable to move a muscle.

Marge Ledbetter blew a shrill blast on her whistle, then pointed toward the faded yellow tents. "Move it. That's an order!"

Rocky and the others sprang into action opening the trunk of the car, tossing the suitcases onto the ground and saying hurried good-byes to Mrs. Bubnik.

"So long, kids." Mary's mother waved one hand out the window. "See you in ten days."

"Ten days?" McGee groaned. "It might as well be ten years." Five miserable girls picked up their belongings and watched as Mrs. Bubnik's old green Volvo disappeared in a cloud of dust down the gravel road.

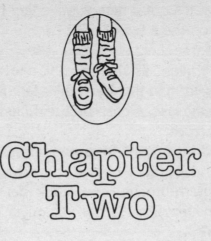

Chapter Two

"This isn't a performing arts camp," Gwen groaned as she stared at the canvas walls of their tent. "This is a boot camp."

"You're telling me." Rocky flopped down on one of the five flimsy wooden beds lining the sides of the tent. Each had a thin mattress, with a pillow, a set of worn sheets, and a khaki wool blanket folded on top. "It's like spending every minute with my father, only worse. At least Dad doesn't make us exercise." Rocky's father ran the Garcia household like his own platoon.

McGee kicked at the worn braided rug covering the center of the wooden platform. "Boy, they really went all out on the decorations here." An old lantern dangled by a rusty chain from the top tentpole. Aside from that, the space was bare.

"At least it's got a nice view," Mary Bubnik said, perching on the edge of her bed.

After Marge Ledbetter had instructed them to "stow their gear," as she called it, under their beds, the counselor had tied back their tent flaps so they could see the lake. A crisp breeze ruffled the surface into little waves.

Zan had been quiet for some time. She stepped outside and carefully circled the drab yellow tent. After a few moments she stuck her head back through the tent flap. "Umm, you guys? Where's our bathroom?"

McGee pulled her baseball cap out of her back pocket and placed it on her head. "They probably have one that we all share. You know, a big brick building, with showers and stuff, like they have in state parks."

Zan shielded her eyes with her hand and squinted off in the distance. "I don't see anything like that. Just the lodge, and a couple of truly tiny shacks nearby."

Gwen, who was busily spraying Buzz Off all over her arms and legs, paused with the can in mid-air. "Tiny shacks?" she repeated. "How tiny?"

Rocky waved her hand in front of her face and coughed. "That stuff is awful." She pulled on her red satin jacket with her name printed in silver on the back, picked up her binoculars, and joined Zan outside. "Those aren't shacks," she said. "Those are latrines."

"What's a latrine?" Mary Bubnik asked, sticking her head out of the tent.

"A latrine is an outhouse," McGee explained as she joined the others.

"That does it!" Gwen shrieked. She grabbed her suitcase from under her bed, flipped up the lid, and tossed her can of bug spray inside. "I'm going home."

"What?" McGee shouted. "You can't."

Gwen snapped the suitcase shut with a bang. "Have you ever been in an outhouse?"

Mary Bubnik and Zan shook their heads.

"They're just holes dug in the ground, with boards across the top."

"So?" McGee asked with a shrug.

Gwen dropped her suitcase to the floor. "So a big, ugly spider or a slimy snake could be hiding in there and one night, when you have to go to the bathroom in the dark, they'll bite you on the bottom."

"That's disgusting," Rocky said, making a face.

"You're telling me." Gwen picked up her suitcase and declared, "That's why I'm going home."

She marched down the two wooden steps of the tent platform and made a beeline for the lodge, with Zan and the others hurrying after her.

"Gwen, get real," McGee said, trotting alongside her. "You can't leave. They won't let you."

"Wanna bet?" Gwen set her chin firmly. "I'm going

13

to tell Marge the Sarge that I have to go home *right now* and I intend to catch the next bus out of here."

"Bus?" Zan repeated. "Gwen, buses don't come way back here."

Gwen paused for a moment to think, then shoved her glasses up on her nose. "So I'll call my mother. When she hears that this place doesn't even have a bathroom, and that my furnished cabin is just a ratty tent with grungy old Army beds, she'll be out here in a flash."

"You can't call," a voice answered from behind them. "For the simple reason that this camp has no phone."

The girls spun around to see a dark-haired girl with thick glasses sitting on a large flat rock. She wore a red sweatshirt with "The Juilliard School of Music" printed on it, and held a clarinet in her hands. Her bony knees stuck out of her dark green shorts like toothpicks in a cucumber.

"I myself discovered that fact only an hour ago," the girl continued in a calm voice, "when I tried to telephone my grandparents. They asked me to let them know when I arrived." She played a quick scale on her clarinet. "I suppose they'll be frantic and call the sheriff."

Gwen looked at her friends, then back at the strange girl. "Good. I hope they do. Then the sheriff can give me a ride to the bus station, and I can get out of this prison camp."

The girl hopped off the rock and strode over to join them. She was all knees and elbows, and she towered over them. Even Zan, who was tall for her age and the tallest of the gang, felt short beside her.

"Then again, my grandmother may assume that if anything has gone awry, the sheriff will call her." The girl shrugged. "It's hard to tell with them." She nodded at Gwen and said, "At any rate, you may have a long wait ahead of you."

Rocky crossed her arms and demanded, "So are you a counselor, or one of us?"

"I'm certainly not a counselor," the girl answered in her clipped way. "But I'm not sure if I'm one of you. What are you?"

"Smokey and the four bears," Rocky retorted. "What does it look like?"

Mary Bubnik tugged on Rocky's sleeve and whispered, "Now be nice." Then she stepped forward. "I'm Mary Bubnik, and these are my friends Gwen, Zan, Rocky, and McGee."

Zan joined her. "We're here to take ballet lessons," she added in her soft voice, "and we're in that tent named Birch."

The tall girl stuck out her hand. "Arvid Epstein. I'm in Cedar."

McGee shook the girl's hand and started to say, "Pleased to meet — "

"I'm from New York," the girl cut in. "I play most of the wind instruments, and am considered a child prodigy."

The gang blinked in amazement as Arvid rattled on.

"Being a musical genius has its ups and downs. I spend quite a bit of time alone. So my grandparents, who I live with, thought it would be a good idea for me to attend a camp with young people my own age to improve my conversational skills."

"Well, I think your conversation is just fine," Mary Bubnik declared in her southern accent. "In fact, you've already used several words that I've never even heard of."

"Why, thank you." Arvid smiled, revealing a mouth full of shiny braces. "I look forward to socializing with each of you." She checked the large watch on her wrist. "But just now I have to get to my next rehearsal."

As Arvid turned and loped down a path into the woods, Rocky whispered, "That girl is too weird for words."

Before any of the others could comment, four blonde girls in identical blue jeans and striped tops stepped out of the tent marked "Aspen." Two of them carried trumpets, one a trombone, and the fourth carried a huge brass tuba.

"Excuse me," the girl with the tuba called out to the gang. "Are you guys musicians?"

McGee shook her head. "We're dancers."

"We're looking for the rehearsal hall," one of the trumpeters explained. "Do you know where it is?"

"No, but we just talked to a girl playing a clarinet

16

who said she had to go to rehearsal," Zan said. She pointed at the path Arvid had taken. "She went that way."

"Thank you."

Mary Bubnik stared at the four blonde girls curiously. "Are y'all sisters?" she blurted out.

"Yes," the one with the tuba answered. "I'm Regina Rand, and this is Rowena, Rafaella, and Rita." Her sisters giggled. Then Rita, who was holding a trombone, whispered something in Regina's ear.

"My sister just said that we'd better find the rehearsal hall," Regina told the gang. "We don't want to be late our first day at camp."

"If you want my opinion," McGee said as they watched the girls disappear, "the Rand Band is as weird as old Arvid Epstein."

"Just one more reason for getting out of here now," Gwen declared.

"Why don't you take a look at the rest of the camp?" Zan suggested. "You haven't even given it a chance."

"Yeah, there may be some really neat things here," Mary Bubnik chimed in.

"Besides, if Arvid's grandparents really do call the sheriff," Rocky said, "it will take a while for him to get here."

McGee nudged Gwen in the ribs. "At least take a look at the lake before you decide."

Gwen looked at the four faces staring at her and slowly nodded. "Okay, I'll go look at the lake." Then

17

she raised her finger in warning. "But the first time I have to go to the bathroom, I'm leaving."

Zan hopped up on a boulder to get her bearings. "This place is truly confusing. Four paths branch off from here but I can't tell where any of them lead."

"They all lead to the same place," a voice said from the other side of the rock. "Lake Chuck."

They scrambled around the rock to find a girl sitting on a log, flipping a stone in the air. This girl had cropped hair dyed black, with little red tips on the ends. She wore blue jeans, a faded black tee shirt, and a leather vest. Her face and arms were tanned as dark as a walnut.

"It's a mile wide, two miles long, fifty feet deep, and there's one scruffy little island in the middle." The girl sighed heavily. "Take any path you like."

"How come you know that?" McGee asked.

"Because I've hiked every trail there is here. I've also swum in the lake, fished from the dock, and climbed all the trees." She tossed the stone at the nearest pine tree. "And that's about all there is to do in this boring place."

"I thought camp only started today," Rocky said.

"It did."

"So how come you know so much about it?"

"I live here," the girl replied. "My parents run the place and I help them."

Gwen narrowed her eyes at her. "Did they print up those brochures?"

"Those old things?" The girl snorted and threw

another rock at the pine tree. "They were printed up twenty years ago — when the camp was a success."

"What is it now?" Mary Bubnik asked with a sinking heart.

"A disaster area. It went broke ten years ago, and my parents took it over." She stood up and brushed the dirt off her jeans. "Now it's a place where a bunch of geeky kids come to play twerpy music."

"I've never played an instrument in my life," Rocky snarled. "And I am not a geek."

The girl shrugged. "I didn't say you were." She picked up a little leather suitcase that had the initials "J.P." printed on it. "I gotta run. Ron's rehearsal starts in five minutes."

"Ron?" McGee repeated.

The girl nodded. "That's my dad. Ron Pulzini — orchestra conductor, and head geek."

"Are you in the orchestra?" Zan asked.

"Sure." She held up a slim black case. "I play the flute. The name's J.P. I'll catch you later."

After J.P. was out of sight, Rocky muttered, "I think we're the only normal kids at this camp."

"And isn't it odd that everyone we've met so far has been in the orchestra?" Zan pointed out.

"Yeah. And I think it's weird that *we* don't have a rehearsal," Rocky added.

"Maybe ol' Leadbottom forgot to tell us about it," McGee said, heading down the path where J.P. had been throwing her rocks. "Come on. Let's check out the lake before someone *does* call us to a rehearsal."

19

"Hold it!" Gwen shouted as they started to move down the center path. She dropped her suitcase on the ground and flipped open the lid.

"You already put a gallon of bug spray on," Rocky said impatiently. "You don't need anymore."

"I'm not getting bug spray," Gwen snapped as she shuffled her clothes around. "I'm looking for my snack supply."

"Snacks?" Mary Bubnik shook her head in dismay. "Gwen, we ate lunch less than an hour ago."

"You call a hot dog and a Coke lunch? I call that an appetizer. Besides, if we're going to hike we're going to need our strength." She held up a bag of M&Ms and two packages of Twinkies. "We don't want to keel over from exhaustion."

Mary Bubnik gasped in alarm. "The brochure said we weren't supposed to bring any sweets. They attract wild animals."

Gwen tore open the bag of candy with her teeth as she hurried down the path with the others. "You heard what J.P. said. That brochure is twenty years old." As the girls clambered up onto an overlook with a clear view of the water, Gwen added, "Besides, all the wild animals are probably long gone by now."

"Says who?" Rocky asked, pulling out her binoculars and scanning the horizon.

"Mary's right, you know," McGee said. "I've heard that bears can smell candy a mile away." She leaned forward to sniff at Gwen, then pinched her nose shut and grimaced. "They also like perfume."

20

"This isn't perfume," Gwen protested. "It's bug spray."

"How's a bear going to know that?" McGee shot back. "It's got the same flowery smell as perfume."

Gwen tossed a handful of M&Ms into her mouth and mumbled, "You guys are nuts. There aren't any bears in Ohio."

"No," Rocky murmured, without taking her eyes off the binoculars. "There's something worse. A lot worse."

"Like what?" Gwen asked.

Rocky shook her head grimly. "I don't believe it."

"What?"

"It's just not possible."

This time they all shouted, *"What?"*

"Look." Rocky handed the binoculars to McGee, who quickly pressed them to her eyes. "Do you see that canoe with Scotsvale painted on the side of it?" Rocky pointed at a little boat that had just circled the tiny island and was heading for their side of the lake.

"Sure. What about it?"

"See those girls in the cute white sailor uniforms having fun?"

McGee nodded again.

"Do they remind you of anybody?"

Suddenly McGee gasped in horror. "No! It can't be. It's . . . it's . . ."

Then McGee and Rocky screamed together, "The Bunheads!"

Chapter Three

Courtney Clay, the leader of the Bunheads, sat in the center of a large wooden canoe. She was wearing a pair of mirrored sunglasses and a white visor. Golden-haired Page Tuttle and mousy little Alice Wescott sat at either end, clutching big wooden paddles in their hands.

Rocky, who had grabbed the binoculars back from McGee, shook her head. "Even at camp they wear their hair in those tight buns. It must just grow that way."

The gang knew Courtney and her friends from the Deerfield Academy of Dance, where they took ballet classes together. From the moment the gang had stepped foot in the academy, Courtney and her friends had seemed bent on making their lives miserable. Their snobby attitude and the way they always wore their hair had earned the Bunheads their nickname.

Zan slumped down on the nearest rock and watched as the sleek canoe cut a path toward their shore. "Of all the camps in the entire country, they have to choose ours. It's just not fair."

"But they're not at our camp," Mary Bubnik protested. "They're at Scotsvale. That's clear across the lake."

"Their camp may be across the lake but the Bunheads are landing on our shore," Gwen said, as the canoe made a beeline for the weathered old dock jutting out from the rocky shore.

"They can't do that!" Rocky protested. Before anyone could say another word, she was halfway to the dock. Rocky didn't bother to take the path. She crashed right down the steep slope through a wild tangle of thorny bushes. She was so upset she didn't even feel where the brambles cut her arms.

"Oh, no, you don't," she shouted, leaping out on the wooden deck with a loud thunk. "This is *our* dock."

Courtney, who was caught with one leg in the canoe and one leg on the dock, lost her balance and nearly fell into the water.

"Help!" she cried, flailing wildly with her arms until Page and Alice reached up and shoved her forward. Finally Courtney grabbed the lone mooring post and hurled herself up onto the dock. She landed heavily

on her knees. "Ouch! I think I got a splinter."

"Serves you right," Gwen called from the edge of the pier. She and the others had taken the path and arrived just in time to see Courtney's fall. "How dare you follow us up here!"

"Follow you?" Courtney repeated as she stood up. "That's a laugh." She folded her arms across her chest and tilted her chin up in a superior way. "For your information, I have been coming to Camp Scotsvale every summer for the past three years. Just like my mother did when she was my age."

"Big wow," McGee drawled.

"Personally, I can't believe Camp Clodhopper is still in existence," Courtney drawled.

Rocky narrowed her eyes at Courtney. "Clodhopper?"

"Of course. Some stupid guy named Claude Harper started it ages ago," Courtney explained in a smug tone, "but it's always been known as Camp Clodhopper to everyone."

"Why is that?" Mary Bubnik asked.

"Because it's full of clods who can't dance or sing," Courtney replied, as Page and Alice snickered loudly from the canoe. "Their parents just send them there to get rid of them for ten days."

"That's not true!" Mary Bubnik shouted. She could feel her chin start to quiver. She had been looking forward to camp for so long, and had worked terribly hard to save her allowance and baby-sitting money, just so she could afford to go. So far, she'd been pretty disappointed by everything, but this was the last straw. "You take that back."

Zan saw Mary's darkening face and stepped forward quickly. "You must be talking about the old Claude Harper Camp," she said. "The one with that metal hut for a lodge, and old tents."

The gang stared at her in total mystification.

"This one is truly different," Zan continued in her logical voice. "It has a brand-new lodge, and big luxurious cabins for all the students."

"That's right," Gwen jumped in. "And each cabin has its own bathroom and sauna."

"Sauna!" Page repeated, suddenly very impressed.

Zan shot Gwen a warning look. She was on the verge of overdoing it. But it was too late, as McGee declared, "And, of course, there are the new tennis courts, softball diamond, and swimming pools."

"Pools?" Alice asked, wide-eyed.

"Sure," Rocky replied. "An outdoor one for good days, and an indoor one for when it rains."

Courtney narrowed her eyes suspiciously. "I don't believe you."

"Oh, and did we mention that the students are mostly from the Juilliard School in New York?" Zan called out, remembering the sweatshirt that Arvid had been wearing.

"That's the best performing arts school in the country," Page gushed.

Mary Bubnik shrugged. "Of course. Camp Claude

Harper only accepts the best students."

"Then what are you guys doing here?" Courtney shot back.

"They're there to show the others what not to do!" Alice cracked.

"Ha ha," Gwen muttered. "Very funny."

Courtney knelt down on the dock and conferred with Alice and Page, who were still in the canoe. Then she straightened up and announced, "We've decided we're going to see this new camp for ourselves."

"Sorry." Rocky linked arms with McGee and Gwen, forming a human chain across the dock. "People from *Snots*vale aren't allowed."

Alice and Page hopped onto the landing and the three Bunheads stood nose-to-nose with Rocky, Gwen, and McGee.

"For your information," Courtney hissed, "Scotsvale owns all the land bordering this lake. Camp Clodhopper just rents their little land. We can go anyplace we want."

"Not if I have anything to say about it." Rocky sprang forward out of the line in a fierce karate pose. She had taken several lessons at the recreation center on the air base — just enough to make her look really threatening.

"Rochelle Garcia!" Courtney howled as the Bunheads backed up nervously. "If you lay one hand on me, I'll scream."

"Who's gonna hear you?" Rocky snorted.

"All our friends across the lake," Alice replied, as she cowered behind Courtney's body.

Rocky looked over her shoulder and called, "Have you got your watch, Zan?"

"Right here, Rocky," Zan replied.

Rocky turned back to face Courtney and pretended to get ready to strike. "Okay, scream. I want to see how long it takes for your friends to paddle over here."

Gwen grinned with pleasure as she watched Courtney squirm. She unwrapped one of her Twinkies and, taking a huge bite, mumbled, "Give 'em a chop for me, Rocky."

Rocky faked a sudden movement and the Bunheads ran screaming for their boat.

"I'm calling my mother," Courtney protested as she battled with Page to get into the canoe first. It dipped dangerously low in the water. "She'll have all of you thrown out of this camp, and out of the ballet academy, and maybe out of the whole state of Ohio."

"Oh, Alice!" McGee sang out. "Did you forget something?"

"What?" Alice snapped, as she stepped gingerly into the canoe after Courtney and Page.

"This!" McGee tossed a small frog that she had scooped up at the water's edge into the canoe. "Catch!"

Alice reached out for the slimy green creature before she knew what it was. The moment her hand touched it, she squealed, "A frog? Get me out of here!" She scrambled into the side of the canoe where Courtney and Page were sitting.

"Oooh, gross!" Courtney clutched at Page, who was scrambling to climb back onto the dock. Meanwhile the frog was flopping around the bottom of the canoe. When it jumped toward the girls, all three of them tried to leap back out of its way. The canoe flipped on its side and dumped them head-first into the water. The frog disappeared out of sight into the lake.

"Way to go!" Rocky crowed, giving McGee a high five.

The water around the dock was only waist deep and Courtney was the first to stand up. Her hair hung limply around her face and her starched sailor suit was sopping wet.

"My brand-new outfit," she wailed. "It's covered with slime!"

Page pushed her dripping wet hair out of her eyes and glared at the gang. "We'll get you for this," she yelled, holding the canoe still as the other two girls struggled to climb back in.

"You'll wish you never came here," Courtney said, as the Bunheads finally managed to find their paddles, and point the canoe back toward the far shore.

McGee and Rocky were laughing so hard, they couldn't respond. Their hoots of laughter followed the Bunheads far out onto the lake.

Mary Bubnik didn't join in. She nibbled nervously

on one nail as she watched the canoe become smaller and smaller, then finally disappear around the island. "Boy, they were awfully mad. Do you think they will *really* try to get us?"

"How?" Rocky asked as she led them up the path back toward the lodge. "They go to their camp, and we go to ours."

Suddenly, an immense shape loomed in the path in front of them, blocking the sun and casting a huge shadow across the startled girls.

"Birch Patrol! Front and center."

Marge Ledbetter was standing with her hands on her hips, looking like a female Hercules. She blew a long blast on her whistle that made their hair stand on end. "You're late, Birch Patrol!"

"For what?" Gwen demanded crossly.

"That's one demerit."

"One demerit?" Gwen repeated. "For what?"

"For talking back to an officer."

"I just asked a question," Gwen protested.

"Two demerits."

"Excuse me, sir?" Mary Bubnik raised her hand. "I mean, ma'am."

Marge Ledbetter nodded curtly. "That's more like it. What's your question, soldier?"

Mary smiled shyly. "Well, actually, I have two."

"Fire away."

"What are we late for? And what does a demerit mean?"

Marge Ledbetter ticked off the questions on her

fingers. "One, you're late for orientation. And two, a demerit is a point. You lose points for being late, keeping a sloppy tent, being rude to a superior — "

Rocky's hand shot up. "What's the punishment?" She pictured the five of them having to dig ditches with spoons, or clean the latrines with toothbrushes, or some other awful torture.

"The tent with the most daily demerits is last into the mess hall to eat," the counselor explained.

"What?" Gwen exploded indignantly. "That's not fair."

Marge Ledbetter pointed her finger at Gwen. "That's three for you."

Gwen started to protest again but McGee and Rocky clapped their hands over her mouth.

The counselor made a note of their demerits on her clipboard. "It may sound unfair but at the Claude Harper Camp, we not only build fine artists but well-mannered young women." She arched a disapproving eyebrow in the direction of Scotsvale. "Unlike *some* camps I know of."

"But I thought — "

Marge Ledbetter blew another loud blast on her whistle. "Double-time to the lodge for orientation. That's where you'll meet the rest of your counselors and campmates."

"I can't wait," Gwen groaned.

Marge Ledbetter opened her mouth to speak when Gwen held up her hand. "I know, I know — four demerits."

30

Chapter Four

When the gang walked into the lodge, they were pleased to see that the inside of the metal hut was much nicer than the outside. Some overstuffed couches and armchairs were scattered in a cozy circle around a woodstove. There was a small stage just beyond the couches at one end of the room. Ten wooden picnic tables were lined up at the other end. The clang of pots and pans could be heard from the open door by the tables, and the aroma of baking bread filled the air. There was a Ping-Pong table along one wall, and an ancient upright piano near the stage, with a dozen or so musical instrument cases stacked beside it.

The orientation meeting was already in progress. A short, plump man with dark hair and glasses was perched on the edge of the stage, talking to a group of about twenty girls, who sat cross-legged on the floor and on the couches. The ancient basset hound who was sleeping on the stage glanced up as the gang walked in.

"I see Sarge found you," the man said, flashing a smile that seemed to stretch from ear to ear. "Come on in and join us. We're all just getting to know each other. I'm Ron Pulzini."

"The conductor," Mary Bubnik whispered knowingly.

"This is Beethoven," Mr. Pulzini announced, scratching the hound behind the ears affectionately. The dog opened one eye and thumped his tail loudly on the stage. Then Mr. Pulzini gestured toward the back of the room. "And that's my wife Trudy in the kitchen."

The girls turned around and saw a jolly woman in a white apron standing in the doorway. A large cooking mitt covered her right hand. She grinned and waved the mittened hand at the girls.

"She's our crafts instructor and chef," Mr. Pulzini explained.

"Each tent will take turns doing KP," Trudy announced. There was a loud groan from all the girls, and Trudy added with a chuckle, "Just be glad that this session is so small. Sometimes our girls have to wash fifty or sixty dishes at a time."

"This really is like boot camp," Rocky grumbled,

as the gang settled themselves on the floor behind the other girls. "The only thing they don't make you do here is march."

A tall, redheaded fellow in a plaid shirt and jeans hopped up on the stage beside Ron and waved. "I'm Harry Hackerwood and I teach poetry. Hopefully, by the end of your time here, I'll have helped you all look at nature in a different light."

"Gee, Gwen," McGee whispered, "Harry's got more freckles than you have."

"I'd like all of you to keep a journal of your experiences here." He patted a stack of black-and-white speckled notebooks lying on a table. "Each of you take one of these, and jot down anything that comes into your head. You'll be surprised at what you come up with."

Zan smiled. She could tell she liked Harry already. "I've been keeping a journal since I was seven," she whispered to the gang.

"I tried keeping a diary," Rocky admitted, "but my brothers kept trying to read it."

"Didn't you lock it up?" McGee asked.

"Sure, but I kept forgetting where I hid the key."

"I got one for my birthday," Mary Bubnik said, "but it got kind of boring. Every day I'd write, 'Went to school, came home, ate dinner, and went to bed.' "

"That *is* boring," Gwen said.

Mr. Pulzini gestured toward the door where Marge

Ledbetter stood. "Of course, you've already met the Sarge."

"Yeah, we've met ol' Leadbottom," Gwen grumbled.

"Leadbottom!" McGee tried to cover her mouth to laugh but ended up snorting loudly and the rest of the campers turned to stare at her. She lowered her hand and added, "That's a good one."

Mr. Pulzini raised an eyebrow in their direction and continued. "She's here to whip us all into shape. Strong bodies and strong minds go together."

"And we're starting first thing tomorrow morning with a brisk swim," Marge Ledbetter bellowed, stepping out in front of the group. "Ten laps — out to the buoy, and back."

"I thought swimming was just for fun," Rocky grumbled.

"This should be lots of fun," Marge Ledbetter said.

"No, I mean I thought we didn't have to do it if we didn't want to."

"Why wouldn't you want to swim?"

The whole room turned to look at Rocky and she felt her face turn beet red. She stared at her hands and tried to think. This was her big chance to admit she couldn't swim. Then the truth would be out in the open and she would be excused. Rocky opened her mouth to speak the truth but strange words came out.

"I love to swim," she heard herself saying. "I just thought other kids might not like it."

Marge Ledbetter looked out at the entire assembly. "Anybody here not like swimming?"

Everyone shook their head.

Marge Ledbetter nodded. "Good. Then I'll see you all at six-thirty sharp."

"In the morning?" Gwen squeaked.

"Of course."

"But won't the water be, um, a little cold?" Mary Bubnik asked.

"A brisk swim at sun-up is just the thing to get the blood running," Marge Ledbetter boomed confidently. "You'll love it."

An uneasy silence fell across the room. The prospect of jumping into a freezing cold lake at dawn sounded positively awful. But no one was going to argue with Marge Ledbetter.

"And last, but not least . . ."

Mr. Pulzini turned and pointed at a thin, dark-haired lady who was sitting in a chair by the edge of the stage. She kept her back held straight as a rod and twisted the handkerchief in her hand into a tight knot.

"I'd like you all to meet Elinor Gretzky," he continued. "Our ballet teacher. This is her first year with us, and I hope it won't be the last."

Miss Gretzky smiled stiffly at the group. "My first class will be here on the stage after dinner," she said. "Um, I guess you know what you are supposed to wear."

The gang looked at each other and nodded confidently. Their standard uniform at the Deerfield

Academy of Dance was black leotards, pink tights, and ballet slippers. The girls had even brought along their toe shoes, in hopes that they would get to practice their *pointe* work.

"Well." Miss Gretzky fumbled with her handkerchief a few more times. "I'll see you this evening, then."

"She seems kind of nervous," Gwen remarked.

"Maybe that's because this is her first year here," Zan suggested. "All of the other counselors have been here before."

"Maybe."

Ron Pulzini leaped off the stage and clapped his hands. "Now, we've got some pretty exciting activities planned for the next nine days," he declared. "My daughter J.P. will tell you about them."

J.P. was in one of the overstuffed chairs by the woodstove, with her legs draped lazily over the arm. "Do I have to?" she asked.

Her father tilted his head down and peered at her over the top of his glasses.

"Okay, okay." J.P. shuffled up to the stage, where her father handed her a clipboard. She took a deep breath. "First, there's the big Sports Face-Off with Camp Scotsvale."

"What's that?" one of the Rand sisters asked. All four of them had crammed themselves onto one couch and were sitting with their hands folded neatly in their laps.

"The Sports Face-Off is a big day of contests," J.P. explained, "where we do things like sack races, softball throws, swimming relays, and basically get creamed by Scotsvale."

"Not this year," Marge declared confidently.

"Wanna bet?" J.P. mumbled. Her father shot her another stern look and she continued to read from the clipboard. "Then we're invited to a dumb bonfire with Scotsvale." She rolled her eyes at the ceiling and announced, "Bo-ring."

"I think I'm going to like her," Gwen murmured.

"She sure doesn't talk like a counselor," Mary Bubnik whispered.

Arvid Epstein, who had been sitting in front of the gang on a plaid cushion on the floor, turned around and whispered, "She's not one. She just helps her parents."

"Oh, and one more thing." J.P. smiled at the group. "There'll be two trail rides led by my good buddy, Teague McBride."

Arvid's eyes widened and she hissed, "I understand from the rest of the campers that he is nothing short of *ultra* cute."

"We saw Teague's horse tied to a truck's bumper," McGee whispered back. "He was a disaster."

"That wasn't Teague's horse," Arvid said with a giggle. "That was Jingles, the camp mascot."

"The perfect choice," Gwen muttered. "A broken-down old nag."

"Teague McBride's horses come from Scotsvale," Arvid explained. "They're really beautiful, too. There's only one small drawback."

"What?" McGee asked.

"The rest of the riders *also* come from Scotsvale."

"Oh, great!" McGee slumped back in her chair.

"Relax," Rocky said, hitting her on the knee. "There were a zillion girls at Scotsvale when we drove by. I bet the Bunheads don't even ride horses."

"Let's hope not," McGee murmured.

"So that's it for now," Mr. Pulzini said, bringing the meeting to a close. "Let's take a break and have some of Trudy's fabulous home cooking."

As everyone around them picked up one of the instrument cases by the piano and headed for the dining tables, Zan said, "I think we're the only dancers at this camp."

"Great," Mary Bubnik said. "That just means we'll be the best!"

"How can you think of dancing at a time like this?" Gwen said.

"What time is it?" McGee asked, confused.

"Chow time. Come on!" Gwen grabbed a plastic tray and headed for the front of the food line. "I'm starved."

"Not so fast, Birch Patrol," Marge Ledbetter barked. "The tent with the most demerits eats last."

"What?" all five of them gasped.

Marge Ledbetter pointed sternly to the end of the line. "Now march!"

After dinner the girls had an hour to themselves before the evening dance class. Gwen took that opportunity to make the first entry in her journal.

Dear Diary,

Camp stinks! Tonight they served us tuna boats for dinner! For your information, a tuna boat is tuna in a taco shell, smothered in cream of mushroom glop. Make me barf! I refused to eat it and Marge the Sarge Leadbottom gave me three demerits. I may starve to death before this week is over.

Miserably yours,
Gwen

Chapter Five

That evening the girls dressed in their leotards and tights and stood on the stage, waiting for their dance teacher. Zan checked her watch. "Our class was supposed to start ten minutes ago."

"Do you think Miss Gretzky ran off?" Mary wondered.

"She's probably as shocked as we are about this place, and is busy trying to hitch a ride back to town," Gwen grumbled.

"She looked kind of nervous," McGee observed.

"Maybe she had to go to the latrine," Rocky suggested.

"And a snake bit her on the bottom," Gwen concluded flatly.

There was a loud crash just outside the door. The gang rushed to see what had happened. They found Elinor Gretzky lying face down on the path, a tape recorder in one hand, and a book titled *Ballet for Beginners* clutched in the other.

"Oh, my goodness," Miss Gretzky mumbled, as she sat up painfully. "I am such a klutz."

"Do you need some help, Miss Gretzky?" Rocky asked, picking up the cassette tapes that had fallen out of their carrying case and were scattered across the ground.

"Thank you." Miss Gretzky smiled gratefully at Rocky and handed her the tape recorder. "Sorry I'm late, girls. I remembered that I'd left all of my equipment back in my tent and — "

"They make the counselors sleep in tents, too?" Gwen blurted in amazement.

"Why, yes." Miss Gretzky got up gingerly and dusted off her black dance skirt.

"That's awful!" Gwen declared. "I'd quit if I were you."

"Oh, mine is quite nice," Miss Gretzky said, flashing a smile that made her look very pretty. "Much better than the stuffy apartment in Cleveland that I shared with my brother and his wife. When the Pulzinis hired me for this job, I was thrilled. My tent may not be plush but at least it's all mine."

The girls greeted their teacher's confession in startled silence. Miss Gretzky giggled nervously, and

41

said, "Well, now you know my life story. What do you say we get started on our class?"

The girls filed back into the lodge and stepped up onto the stage. Miss Gretzky followed behind them, flipping hurriedly through the front of her book. "We don't have a real ballet *barre* because it's being repaired," she said, "but this manual suggests we use the backs of chairs."

Rocky spotted some folding chairs stacked against the wall. "Will these do?"

"Perfect."

Each of the girls grabbed a chair and placed them in a semi-circle on the floor. Miss Gretzky set the tape recorder on the floor and announced, "All right, now where should we begin?"

The gang looked at each other in confusion. Finally McGee cleared her throat and said, "Well, at our school in Deerfield, we usually start with *pliés.*"

"An excellent idea!" Elinor clapped her hands together gleefully. "Why don't you lead us all in them?"

"Okay," McGee replied with a shrug. "Um, let's do two *demi-pliés,* one *grand plié,* and then two more *demi-pliés* with *relevés.*" McGee demonstrated by bending her knees and then raising up onto half *pointe.* "We'll finish with a *port de bras* over to the floor, touching your nose to your knee —"

"Fat chance," Gwen cracked.

"Then we'll do that in all five positions," McGee concluded.

"Say, you're good," Miss Gretzky said, patting McGee on the back.

McGee flipped one braid over her shoulder. "Thanks."

Miss Gretzky pressed a button on the tape recorder and McGee led the gang in their warm-ups. After they'd finished, Miss Gretzky applauded appreciatively. "Very, very good. Now, what would the teachers at your academy have you do next?

The gang exchanged bewildered glances. This time it was Rocky who spoke up. "Well, we generally do some *tendus*." She pointed her foot in front of her and then folded it back into fifth position. "You know — front, side, back, side."

Gwen raised her hand. "Then we add a *rond de jambe.*"

Miss Gretzky cocked her head and Zan explained, "That means 'round the leg,' in French." She pointed her foot in front of her, then drew a half-circle on the floor, moving her leg from front to back.

"Very impressive," Miss Gretzky said. "Shall we continue?" She hit the button on the tape recorder again and the girls took turns leading the warm-ups.

After they had finished, Miss Gretzky told them to fold up their chairs and return them to the stack in the corner.

"And now for the fun part — the floor work," Miss

Gretzky declared. "This is the part where you can really let yourself go."

Miss Gretzky's enthusiasm was impossible to resist. With a shout the gang raced to one end of the stage. "What should we do?" McGee asked eagerly.

"Why don't we play Follow the Leader?" Miss Gretzky suggested. "Each of you do your favorite ballet move across the floor, and everyone else will imitate you."

"Great!" Rocky liked doing the *channé* turns, so she lined up first. "Follow me," she ordered the rest, as she spun like a top across the wooden platform to the other side.

"Can we *chassé* next?" Mary Bubnik squealed. "*Chassé* means 'chase,'" she explained to Miss Gretzky. "One foot tries to catch up with the other." She giggled and added, "It's really funny 'cause we always used this step when we were little kids pretending to ride horses."

"Oooh, let me see it!" Miss Gretzky cried with a delighted clap of her hands. "And throw in your horse moves."

Mary Bubnik galloped across the floor, slapping her thighs and yelling, "Giddy up!" at the top of her lungs. The others followed suit, laughing the entire way.

Miss Gretzky put on waltz music and Zan led them in *balancés* across the floor. Then Gwen suggested they do her favorite step, the *bourrée*.

"It's really pretty easy," she told Miss Gretzky. "You

44

just raise up on your toes, and take little tiny steps across the floor. The only hard part is keeping your stomach sucked in."

"Well, you look like you are just floating on air," Miss Gretzky said after Gwen had covered the length of the stage.

Gwen blushed with pleasure. She couldn't remember the last time a ballet teacher had given her a compliment.

McGee finished off the class with a series of *grands jetés.* They all followed her in a circle, bellowing, "Run, run, *leap!* Run, run, *leap!*"

When the music stopped, all five girls collapsed in a heap of giggles on the floor. Miss Gretzky joined them, laughing just as hard as the gang.

"Boy, that's the most fun ballet class I've ever had," Mary Bubnik declared.

"I really enjoyed it, too," Miss Gretzky said. "You girls are terrific!"

They beamed at each other proudly.

"Is there anything we should work on for tomorrow?" Mary Bubnik asked, as Miss Gretzky gathered up her tape recorder, tapes, and book.

"Tomorrow I have a surprise for you." Miss Gretzky lowered her voice conspiratorially. "Teague McBride is leading a trail ride from Camp Scotsvale, and I've arranged for you girls to go along."

"Great!" McGee clapped her hands together. She couldn't wait to get on a horse.

"Will you come along?" Gwen asked.

45

"Oh, no. I'll be here, catching up on my reading." Miss Gretzky patted the book cradled in her arm.

"Then is there anything we should work on for the next day?" Mary Bubnik asked.

"The next day?" Miss Gretzky looked confused.

"We're supposed to have class every day," Zan reminded her.

"Oh, that's right," the teacher giggled. "Let me see." She put one finger to her lips thoughtfully. "Why don't you each bring in a new step, one that we didn't do today, and we'll try it out." She started to leave and then added, "I can't wait to see what you'll show me. You girls really are wonderful."

After the door shut, Mary Bubnik gushed, "She is the nicest ballet teacher we've ever had."

"And that was the most fun I've ever had in class," Gwen declared.

"The best part was that she let us talk all the way through," McGee added. "The teachers at the Academy are always so strict about that."

"I bet she'd even let us wear shorts to class," Rocky said. "And let our hair down, too." She yanked the rubber band off her ponytail and her wild black hair burst into a cloud around her face.

Gwen noticed that Zan was being awfully quiet. "What's the matter, Zan?" she asked. "Didn't you like our class?"

"I truly loved our class," Zan admitted. "But didn't you notice something strange about our new teacher?"

46

"What, that she's a klutz?" Gwen cracked, remembering Miss Gretzky's tumble on the sidewalk outside.

Zan nodded without smiling. "That, and . . ." She took a deep breath and looked intently at the group. "She doesn't know a thing about ballet."

Chapter Six

The rusty old blue pick-up truck trailed a thick plume of dust as it pulled through the heavy stone gates of Camp Scotsvale the next afternoon. Harry Hackerwood was at the wheel while the gang sat with Arvid Epstein on canvas tarps in the back. She was the only other girl from their camp who'd signed up for the trail ride.

The pick-up truck sputtered and belched up the winding road toward the stables. Some of the Scotsvale girls made a big show of coughing from the smoky exhaust and casting dirty looks at the truck.

"Welcome to Camp Snotsvale," Rocky said sourly.

When they arrived, a lean boy with sunstreaked hair was riding a beautiful Appaloosa horse around the corral.

"That's him!" Arvid squealed.

"Him who?" Gwen demanded.

"Teague McBride," Arvid replied, collapsing in a heap on the floor of the truck bed. "Everything anyone has ever said about him is true," she gushed. "I don't think I can ride now, I'll be too nervous."

"He sure is cute," Mary Bubnik agreed, hurriedly trying to smooth down her curly blonde hair, which had been mussed by the wind.

"I wonder how old he is," McGee said out loud as she watched the handsome wrangler expertly round up a few stray horses and lead them into the stable.

"Sixteen," Arvid called from down on the floor. "He's from Yellow Springs, Ohio. His parents own a farm just outside of town, and he works as a wrangler in the summers to save money for college."

"How do you know all that?" Rocky demanded.

Arvid raised her head over the side of the truck to peer cautiously at the blond boy on the spotted horse. "Research. My grandparents insisted on a detailed report of every counselor's background before they agreed to let me come."

Gwen pushed up her glasses. "You mean, they *knew* about the conditions at our camp?"

Arvid nodded. "The rustic setting is what appealed to them." Then she smiled, and the bright sunlight glinted off her full set of braces. "They're from New York City, so they think outhouses are quaint."

"Have they ever had to use one?" Gwen asked.

Harry Hackerwood brought the truck to a stop and

49

flicked off the ignition. The motor coughed and rat-tled for a full minute before it finally died. "Everybody out!" Harry called from inside as he banged at the door with his shoulder to get it open.

"I don't believe it." McGee pointed to the stable where three beautiful horses trotted into the after-noon sunlight. The lead horse was a palomino with a long blond mane and a tail that nearly touched the ground.

Courtney Clay sat primly on the horse's back, per-fectly dressed in traditional tan riding breeches and tall black boots. She wore a white turtleneck jersey and sported a black velvet riding helmet on top of her bun. A long riding crop dangled from her left hand.

Page Tuttle and Alice Wescott were riding a pair of gray horses behind Courtney, and they looked like carbon copies of her.

Courtney nudged her horse in the side with the heel of her boot, and the animal trotted up to the side of the truck.

"Well, if it isn't the Misfits," she purred. "Late as usual." She waved her hand airily at the truck. "And what is this? Your limousine?"

There was a loud wrenching sound as Harry finally got the door to open. "Never judge a book by its cover," he said, climbing down to the ground. "Over the years this baby has helped a lot of our campers out of jams." He patted the hood of the truck affec-tionately. "If something went wrong on your trail ride today, old Blue here would be the only vehicle able to reach you."

Courtney tossed her head. "What could possibly go wrong? I've been riding English since I was seven." She cast a scornful glance at the gang as they climbed down from the back of the truck. "The only people you'll need to worry about is them."

"Boy, is she a snot," Arvid whispered to Rocky, who answered, "You said it."

Page trotted her gray horse up beside Courtney. "Perfect day for a trail ride, don't you think?"

"Dee-lightful," Gwen said between clenched teeth.

"Wait'll you guys see your horses," Alice Wescott said in her nasal voice. "They're really neat."

"Gee," Mary Bubnik whispered to Rocky, "Page and Alice are being awfully nice."

"Yeah. Too nice," Rocky grumbled. "Something must be up."

"Look! Teague's bringing out our horses!" McGee cried. She and Zan hopped out of the truck and ran over to the barn door to watch the horses parade by.

"They're truly beautiful," Zan breathed softly.

Teague led the string of saddled horses into the corral and lined them up along the fence.

"Howdy, girls," Teague called as he hopped off his horse's back. "Ready for a trail ride?"

"You bet!" The gang lined up in front of the wrangler and waited eagerly for him to assign each of them a horse.

"Who wants to be first to saddle up?"

The girls all pointed to McGee. "She does."

"McGee's our expert," Mary Bubnik added with a giggle.

"Okay, then why don't you ride Bob? He's that big bay at the end of the line."

McGee took a look at the horse named Bob and swallowed hard. The dark brown horse had a long black mane and tail and was larger by far than any of the other horses.

"Excuse me?" McGee asked quietly. "Don't you have something in a, um, smaller size?"

"Oh, don't be intimidated by Bob," Teague replied. "He's really very gentle. Sometimes I give Cheyenne a break and ride him myself."

McGee just stared at Bob and shook her head. "He's just so . . . so *huge*."

Gwen and Rocky exchanged worried glances. It was clear McGee was petrified of the gigantic horse.

Rocky grabbed McGee by the arm and pulled her off to one side. "I thought you said you'd ridden before," she whispered in McGee's ear.

"I have," McGee replied, "but they were much smaller horses. Besides, they were attached to those little metal merry-go-rounds at the carnival."

"You're talking about those pony rides that only go in a circle," Gwen whispered in amazement.

"Don't tell the Bunheads that," McGee said hurriedly. "They'll never let me live it down."

"Look, McGee," Rocky suggested, "why don't I

52

ride Bob, and you can have that little pinto over there."

"What's the matter, McGee?" Courtney taunted. "Scared?"

McGee tossed her head defiantly. "Of course not." She marched up boldly to the horse and patted him on the nose. "Good boy, Bob, good boy." She ran her hand along the horse's neck and lifted her leg toward the stirrup.

Suddenly, all of the Bunheads burst into laughter. "Look, she's getting on the wrong side of the horse."

McGee's eyes widened and she quickly ducked under the horse's neck. "I was just petting him." Then she called loudly to Teague, "Does Bob like to gallop?"

"He loves it," Teague replied.

"Good," McGee said, slipping her foot in the stirrup and reaching for the saddle horn. "Because I love to *ruuuuuuuhnnnnnnnnnnnnn!*"

Her last word turned into a scream as the saddle suddenly slipped sideways beneath her weight. The sound of McGee's scream and the stirrup flapping against his leg startled Bob and he bolted forward.

"Yikes!" McGee struggled to free her foot from the stirrup and fell back heavily on the ground. Bob circled the paddock twice before charging out through the open gate. He headed at full gallop into the woods with his saddle flapping upside down beneath his belly.

Teague leaped onto his horse and rode full tilt after the runaway horse.

Courtney, Page, and Alice couldn't stop laughing. "Boy, Bob sure does like to run!" Page cracked.

"Too bad you couldn't join him, McGee," Courtney added.

"I'm not getting on a horse if the saddle does that," Gwen declared nervously.

McGee got to her feet, angrily dusting off her legs and checking her skinned elbow. "The saddle only does that if someone loosens it. On purpose." She glared at Courtney.

A few minutes later Teague galloped back to the barn, leading Bob by the bridle.

"I don't know how that happened," he told the girls. "I'm sure I tightened all the cinches." He looped Bob's reigns securely around the hitching post. "Just to be on the safe side, I'm going to recheck everybody's saddle."

"I've already tested mine," Rocky said, as she stuck her foot in the stirrup of the chestnut horse she'd chosen.

"Fine. You've picked a good horse," Teague said, coming over to give her a boost up. "This one's name Sweet Sioux."

Rocky looped one leg across Sweet Sioux's back and settled into the saddle. The moment Rocky sat down, Sweet Sioux flared her nostrils and flattened her ears back against her head. With a neigh that sounded like a shriek, the horse leaped into the air.

"Sioux!" Teague bellowed. "What's got into you, girl?"

The horse snorted angrily as she spun in a circle, kicking her legs out behind her.

"She must not like her rider," Courtney said loudly to Page, who giggled even more.

Alice Wescott cupped her hands around her mouth and hollered, "Ride 'em, cowboy!"

In the meantime Zan was shouting, "Hold on, Rocky!" while Gwen was screaming, "Rocky, jump off!"

Rocky didn't hear any of them. All of her attention was focused on keeping her arms wrapped tightly around Sweet Sioux's neck and hanging on for dear life. She squeezed her eyes shut and yelled, "Whoa, horse. Whoa!"

Teague's movements were lightning quick. With one hand he grabbed Sweet Sioux's reins, then looped his other arm around Rocky's waist and scooped her out of the saddle. As soon as Rocky was off Sweet Sioux, the horse stopped bucking.

"I don't get it," Teague murmured. He uncinched the horse's saddle and, lifting it off her back, slid his hand beneath the maroon blanket.

"Aha! Here's the problem!" He pulled out a large thorny burr. "It must have accidentally caught on the blanket in the last trail ride, and I didn't notice it when I saddled up poor Sioux this morning."

"That was no accident," McGee muttered. "Some-body put it there on purpose."

"How could they have known we were going to be on this trail ride?" Gwen whispered.

"Easy." Zan pointed to the sign-up sheet posted on the barn door. "Our names are right there on the list."

Teague resaddled the horse and then called to Rocky, "Want to try again?"

Rocky wanted to say no, but after looking at the Bunheads, who were smiling smugly, she said, "Sure!"

Teague gave McGee and Rocky a boost onto their horses' backs. Then he introduced Gwen, Zan, Mary, and Arvid to their horses.

"This one here is named Brownie." He affectionately slapped a pudgy, little quarter horse on the rump. "You can tell he's got a real sweet tooth."

"That reminds me," Gwen said, digging in the pocket of her windbreaker and producing a plastic bag. "I brought along some trail mix in case we got hungry. I wonder if Brownie would like some."

She opened the bag, scooped up a handful, and held it out to the horse, who snapped it up eagerly.

"That doesn't look like any trail mix I've ever seen," Arvid said as she struggled to get onto her own horse, a tall gray mare named Misty. "What's in it?"

"It's my own special blend." Gwen popped another handful in her mouth, and then fed some more to Brownie. "M&M's, cashews, and Gummi Bears."

Brownie ate the handful and then came back for

more. This time he yanked the plastic bag out of Gwen's hand.

"Hey!" she shouted. "Give that back!"

"Brownie thinks you should go on a diet," Alice cracked.

Gwen ignored Alice and after wrestling with the short, plump horse, finally managed to jerk the remains of the bag out of his mouth. She quickly tucked it into her pocket and, with some help from the wrangler, got on Brownie's back.

Teague lifted Mary onto a black-and-white pinto named Toby and then the wrangler gave Zan a leg up onto another pinto.

"This horse is named Half Moon," Teague explained, "because of the white blaze on his face. But everybody just calls him Moon. Moon's slow, but he's steady."

"That's truly fine with me," Zan said, relaxing a little in the saddle. After witnessing Bob's run through the woods and Rocky's wild ride, she had been having serious second thoughts about getting on any horse.

"All right, pardners," Teague shouted, as he swung onto Cheyenne's back. "Let's head 'em up, and move 'em out!"

Teague guided Cheyenne toward the gate and the other horses automatically fell in line behind the lead horse. The horses were anxious to get going and they trotted spiritedly out of the corral and down a wooded trail toward the lake.

Toby's trotting jostled Mary Bubnik up and down so hard her teeth knocked together. "This-is-just-like-be-ing-in-a-ce-ment-mix-er," she said between bounces.

Gwen's horse Brownie was thoroughly enjoying his ride, largely because Gwen handed him a handful of trail mix every few feet. "My horse is the greatest," she called as she leaned across his neck and hugged him. "I wonder if he likes pizza?"

Teague led them out of the woods into an open meadow of tall grass. The horses took that as a signal to pick up the pace and suddenly all of them were galloping through the meadow along the lake.

"How do you steer this thing?" Zan cried as she clung to the saddle horn with both hands. She'd completely let go of Moon's reins and they flapped against his neck as he raced along.

Teague turned around in his saddle and shouted, "Hold onto the reins. You pull to the right for a right turn, and to the left for a left turn."

"What do I do to get him to slow down?" Zan called.

This time Courtney turned and yelled, "Pull back hard."

Zan scooped up the trailing reins and pulled back with all her might. Moon instantly locked his knees and came to a dead stop. It was so abrupt that Zan nearly tumbled over the top of his head.

Behind her, Gwen's horse did the exact same thing. "I didn't give the whoa command," Gwen

58

muttered in confusion. "Why did he stop?"

"Because mine did," Zan said.

"Look, the others are getting away from us." Gwen pointed to the line of riders far in front of them. "Tell Moon to giddy up."

Zan leaned forward and spoke very clearly into her horse's ear. "Giddy up."

Moon cocked his ear back to listen, then lowered his head and tore off a huge mouthful of grass. Brownie did the same.

Gwen folded her arms across her chest. "How can he be hungry, when he's eaten my entire supply of trail mix?"

Zan shrugged. "Maybe they'll just have a quick snack and then join the others." She raised her hand to shield the sun from her eyes and stared down at the lake while Moon and Brownie lazily tugged at clumps of grass and munched happily.

Gwen slid off Brownie's back and landed heavily on the ground. "I think we should just walk them down to join the others." She pulled hard at the reins. "Come on, Brownie." The horse locked his knees stubbornly. "He won't budge. What do we do?"

"I don't know," Zan said as she hopped off Moon and tugged at his reins. "Just wait for the others to come back, I guess."

Meanwhile, far up ahead, Teague had brought the rest of the party to a stop at the water's edge. They lined up in a half-circle, staring out at the deep blue water.

59

"That's Wild Horse Island," Teague said, pointing to a tiny island far out on the lake. "I stay in a cabin out there."

"Aren't you lonely out there by yourself?" Courtney asked, inching her horse close to the handsome boy.

"I've got my dog, and there are lots of squirrels and chipmunks to keep me company."

As he spoke, Mary Bubnik's horse nosed in between Teague and Courtney.

Courtney twisted in her saddle and narrowed her eyes at Mary. "Back off, will you?"

"Don't look at me," Mary Bubnik protested. "Talk to Toby."

Courtney dug in the pocket of her vest and produced a carrot. "I wonder if Toby would like a snack?"

Mary Bubnik smiled. "I'm sure he'd love one. Thanks."

She reached for the carrot but Courtney raised it above her head and the moment Teague turned his back, tossed it into the lake.

"There, Toby," Courtney whispered. "Fetch!"

Before Mary or anybody knew what was happening, Toby had lunged into the water up to his belly. Mary Bubnik looked back at the others and giggled, "Look, my horse likes to go wading."

"Oh, no!" Teague said, leaping off Cheyenne and rushing into the water. "Can you swim?"

"Why?" Mary asked innocently.

"Because Toby likes to — "

Splash!

Teague finished his sentence as the horse fell sideways. "Roll over."

Rocky screamed as she watched Mary fly off the saddle and fall into the water. Her cry startled McGee's horse, who reared up and turned toward the path leading back to the stables. He was off like a shot, totally ignoring McGee's attempts to stop him. Arvid and Rocky held on for dear life as their horses followed right after McGee.

Zan and Gwen barely had time to jump off the path as the horses thundered by.

"What's going on?" Zan cried.

"It's a stampede!" McGee shouted but her words were lost in the sound of pounding hoofs.

When they saw the other horses, Brownie and Moon stopped grazing and raised their heads. With a loud whinny they joined in the mad gallop back to the barn.

"Wait!" Gwen and Zan chased after their horses through the tall grass.

Meanwhile, on the lawn by the stables, Scotsvale was having a croquet tournament. The players paused in mid-swing as McGee burst out of the woods, struggling madly to bring her horse under control. Rocky and Arvid were right behind her.

The three horses pounded past the startled crowd into the paddock. When they reached the water trough, the horses stopped cold.

Forty girls watched as McGee, Rocky, and Arvid

soared over their horses' necks and landed head-first in a huge pile of hay and manure.

Seconds later, two riderless horses galloped across the playing field. Then Zan and Gwen stumbled out of the woods and collapsed in front of the crowd, gasping for breath.

Finally, Teague appeared, leading Toby by the halter. Mary Bubnik sat miserably on the horse's back. She was sopping wet and covered with mud from head to toe.

Teague reined Cheyenne to a halt by the water trough and then hopped off. While Zan and Gwen helped Rocky, McGee, and Arvid out of the manure pile, Teague lowered Mary to the ground. "You girls all right?" he asked.

None of them could look at him. They were too embarrassed. They just nodded.

"I'm glad to hear it."

The wrangler began rounding up their horses as the Bunheads trotted into the paddock. Courtney expertly guided her palomino up to the girls and announced in a voice that echoed around the camp, "Before you sign up for another trail ride at Camp Scotsvale, I suggest you learn how to ride."

The gang stood staring at the ground as the mocking laughter of forty girls filled their ears.

Chapter Seven

ROCKY'S !!*PRIVATE*!! JOURNAL
KEEP OUT! (This means *YOU!*)

Camp. Day Three, and I'm already running out of excuses for not going swimming. I feel so stupid. Everyone, including J.P. Pulzini and the weirdo Rand sisters, can swim. Why didn't anybody teach me? I also can't ride a horse — but neither can anybody else. Last night we sang around the campfire and the Pulzini family played a whole song on flutes. It was pretty. Then the first star came into

*the sky and everyone closed their eyes
and made a wish. I wished I could swim.*
                                    Rocky

P.S. If anybody *reads this, they're dead!*

"Birch Patrol!" a voice bellowed outside their tent the next morning. "Front and center for inspection."

Rocky quickly stuffed her journal beneath the thin mattress and threw her red satin jacket on over her pajamas. Four bleary-eyed girls stumbled out onto the grass in front of the tent. Zan and Mary Bubnik were still in their flowered nightgowns while McGee had managed to pull on a pair of shorts under her nightshirt.

"Where's the fifth one?" Marge Ledbetter barked. "Gwendolyn Hays?"

"In here," a muffled voice answered. "I'm stuck."

Marge Ledbetter threw back the tent flap and gasped at the sight before her. The girls' riding clothes from the previous day were strewn all over the floor. None of the beds had been made. McGee's mattress was half on the floor because her foot had gotten caught in the blankets when she'd scrambled out of bed.

In the middle of the entire mess lay Gwen, completely tangled up in mosquito netting. "Get me out of here," she yelled, struggling against the thin material. "I feel like a mummy."

Marge Ledbetter picked her way through the pile

of clothes, grabbed hold of one end of the netting, and flipped it open like she was unrolling a carpet. Gwen sprawled out onto the floor with a thunk.

"I'm free," she groaned feebly.

The counselor loomed above Gwen with her hands on her hips. "I guess you know what this means."

Gwen lifted her head. "Four demerits?"

Marge Ledbetter shook her head. "Five."

Gwen flopped back against the floor with a loud groan. "The last to eat again."

Then Marge Ledbetter put the whistle to her lips and blew a shrill blast that made them cover their ears. "Now I want this cabin spotless, and then I want to see all of you down at the lake for lap swimming."

"Swimming?" Rocky, who'd stuck her head through the open tent flap, suddenly fell back onto the ground, clutching her leg. Zan and Mary Bubnik raced to her side.

"Rocky, what is it?" Zan cried.

"Trail ride," Rocky groaned loudly. "Bucking bronco. Oh, the pain, the pain!" She rocked back and forth, trying to look like she was in agony.

"Do you need to see Trudy?" Marge Ledbetter asked, emerging from the tent. Trudy Pulzini, besides being the crafts instructor, cook, and bookkeeper, was also the camp nurse. "Maybe it's broken."

"It's not broken," Rocky said quickly, sitting up. "I just need to keep it elevated." She remembered a doctor telling her to do that when she'd sprained her ankle playing kickball at school.

"Well, see that you do," Marge Ledbetter ordered.

"Gosh, Rocky," Mary Bubnik said, kneeling beside her, "yesterday you had that upset stomach, and now you've got a hurt leg. At this rate you'll never go swimming."

"That's the idea," Rocky muttered under her breath.

The day before she had pretended to be sick from eating tunafish and it had worked. Marge Ledbetter had even felt sorry for her and brought her a can of 7-Up to settle her stomach.

"Gee, Sarge," Rocky said, looking up at the counselor, "I feel just awful about this, especially since swimming is my favorite sport."

"That's all right, Garcia," Marge Ledbetter said, ruffling Rocky's hair. "You just get better. There'll be plenty more chances for you to get in the water."

Rocky smiled weakly. That was the last thing she wanted to hear.

Then Marge Ledbetter turned to face the other four girls. "The rest of you, pick up this mess, and then suit up!"

"Yes, sir!" All four of them snapped to attention, then added, "I mean, ma'am!"

"In the meantime, Garcia, head on over to the kitchen and put some ice on that leg. If you feel better, why don't you try a couple of *pirouettes,* or whatever it is you dance-types do in class. We wouldn't want you to get flabby." Marge Ledbetter patted her own stomach. It sounded like she was hitting a board. "Remember, a fit body means a fit mind."

66

"Yes, sir — I mean, ma'am. I'll do that."

"Good." Marge Ledbetter nodded her approval.

Rocky hopped out of the tent and limped as convincingly as she could toward the lodge.

But when she got there, Rocky veered quickly to the right, threw open the door to the gardening shed, and nearly passed out from fright. Someone was already in there. Rocky was about to scream when a shaft of sunlight reflected off a pair of braces.

"Arvid?" she said, opening the wooden door wide. "What are you doing in here?"

The tall gawky girl sat cross-legged on a stack of bags filled of peat moss. "I'm meditating. Please be so good as to shut the door."

"Why aren't you swimming laps?" Rocky demanded.

"I'm allergic to water."

"Oh." Rocky started to close the door, then stopped. "Wait a minute. Nobody's allergic to water."

"Look," Arvid hissed, "either come in, or close the door. I don't want ol' Leadbottom to see me."

"She won't." Rocky stepped inside the shed and pulled the door shut behind her. "I just talked to her and she's gone to the lake."

"That's a relief." Arvid relaxed and leaned back against the wooden wall. Little streams of light filtered in through the knotholes in the wood and Rocky could clearly see Arvid's face.

"What would happen if Sarge found you?" Rocky asked.

"She'd make me swim," Arvid said, "and I can't."

"You're kidding!" Rocky gasped.

"I don't joke about serious matters like that."

Rocky was relieved to find she wasn't alone and her terrible secret came blurting out. "I can't, either."

Arvid flashed a smile, revealing her full set of braces, and stuck out her hand. "Welcome to the club."

Rocky shook her hand and flopped down on an overturned pail. "I thought everyone knew how to swim but me."

"I'm from New York City," Arvid explained. "No one in New York City knows how to swim. What's your excuse?"

Rocky wrapped her arms around her knees. "I have four brothers. Every time I tried to learn, they made fun of me or dunked me. So I just stopped getting in the water."

Arvid nodded sagely. "I understand."

Rocky picked up a handful of gravel from the dirt floor of the shed and let it trickle through her fingers. "So what are we going to do?"

"Well, I guess we could just 'fess up," Arvid suggested.

Suddenly the door burst open and Rocky sprang to her feet in alarm. It was Miss Gretzky, clutching a flashlight in one hand and her *Ballet for Beginners* in the other.

"What are you doing in here?" Miss Gretzky asked, a startled look on her face.

68

"Hiding from ol' Leadbottom," Rocky blurted out. Then she caught herself and stammered, "I-I mean, Miss Ledbetter."

A tiny smile crossed the teacher's face. "Why would you be hiding from her?"

Rocky and Arvid exchanged looks, then turned and said solemnly, "We can't swim."

"I see." Miss Gretzky studied their faces.

Rocky and Arvid held their breaths, waiting for her to turn them in.

Finally Miss Gretzky whispered, "Don't worry. I'll never tell." Then she stepped inside the shed and added, "If you'll keep my secret."

"What is it?" Rocky asked in a whisper.

"I can't dance."

"I knew it!" Rocky said, snapping her fingers. "Then how did you get this job?"

"Well, actually, I *can* dance," Miss Gretzky explained, "I just never studied ballet." She lowered her voice mysteriously. "My specialty is something quite different."

Rocky's eyes widened. "What?"

Miss Gretzky tossed the ballet book and flashlight onto a pile of burlap sacks in the corner. She kicked one leg high in the air, spun backwards in a tight circle, and struck a dramatic pose with both arms raised above her head. "Flamenco!"

Chapter Eight

"One, two, and three!"

Miss Gretzky clapped her hands together in time with the music coming from her tape recorder, while the girls practiced their very first steps of flamenco dancing.

When the gang had joined Rocky at the lodge after swimming, she'd told them the good news. "This summer we're going to learn a new type of dance — stomping cockroaches!"

They were swirling around the stage, trying to follow Miss Gretzky's instructions. The fiery strumming of the Spanish guitar grew faster and faster.

"I really like dancing in high heels," Mary Bubnik declared, as she raised up on her toes and brought her heels down hard on the floor in time with Miss

Gretzky's count. "One, two, and *three!*"

Miss Gretzky had found enough pairs of black dance shoes in the camp's costume racks to fit all of them. Most of them had a two-inch heel with a buckle strap across the top.

Zan lifted her foot and looked down glumly at the high-heeled shoe. "These make me tower over everyone. I feel like a giant."

Miss Gretzky heard Zan's words and stopped the music. "A giant? Oh, no, no, no, Zan — you must feel like a goddess!"

Suddenly Zan felt very self-conscious and she slumped over even more. "I thought we were going to study ballet," she said, folding her arms across her chest. "Now we're parading around in high heels. We could break our ankles."

The girls stared at Zan in shock. She was usually the last to complain about anything.

Rocky came up and put her arm around her friend. "Look, Zan, just think of this as a new mystery you have to solve." Rocky knew Zan's passion was reading mysteries — especially the adventures of *Tiffany Truenote, Teen Detective.*

"You're talking about a book," Zan protested. "This is a dance. One that I don't have a clue about."

"Ah!" Miss Gretzky hit her forehead with the heel of her hand. "I realize what I've done wrong. I've gotten ahead of myself. In order to dance flamenco, you must *think* flamenco."

"We studied Spanish at my school in Oklahoma,"

71

Mary Bubnik said. "But my teacher never mentioned flamenco dancing."

Miss Gretzky laughed merrily. "No, what I mean is you must know what a flamenco dancer feels inside."

"What does she feel?" McGee asked, flipping one braid over her shoulder.

Miss Gretzky grabbed the hem of her black wrap-around skirt and put her hands on her hips. "First of all, a flamenco dancer is a woman who is not afraid to be wild." She threw her head back for emphasis.

"You mean, like scream and yell and make faces?" Mary Bubnik asked.

Miss Gretzky cocked her head slightly. "Sort of. Here, I'll show you." She reached up and removed a few pins from her dark hair, which had been coiled in a bun at her neck. It tumbled down in long waves to her waist. "Let's start by letting our hair down."

Gwen patted her short, straight bob, which was still damp from swimming, and grimaced. "Mine's as down as it's going to get."

"Then take off your glasses," Miss Gretzky instructed. "And prepare to let loose!"

Gwen removed her wire-rimmed glasses and carefully set them on one of the folding chairs. At the same time, McGee undid her braids and her thick chestnut hair fell about her shoulders. Mary Bubnik removed the pink bow-shaped barrettes holding back her blonde curls.

With a sigh, Zan slipped off her headband and joined the others, who stood facing Miss Gretzky expectantly.

"We're ready to be wild," Rocky declared as she yanked the rubber band out of her hair.

"Good." Miss Gretzky started the music once again. "Each of you, shake your head back and forth with the music."

As the music pounded rhythmically, the girls flopped their heads from side to side.

"Now spin in a circle, and let your arms fly free," Miss Gretzky instructed. "Pretend we are dancing around a roaring campfire and we are becoming part of the flames."

As the girls spun and twirled, Gwen moaned, "My Cheerios are sloshing against my orange juice, and it doesn't feel too good."

Miss Gretzky clapped her hands together for them to stop. "Very good! You all look wonderfully wild and free. Now slow down, and strut around the room with your chin held high, as if you were better than everyone else."

"Like the Bunheads," McGee cracked, imitating Courtney Clay perfectly.

The girls burst into giggles and Miss Gretzky ordered, "Don't smile."

"Aren't we supposed to be wild and happy?" Zan asked.

"A flamenco dancer is fire and ice." Miss Gretzky arched her neck and stared down at them intensely, her dark eyes alight with a passionate gleam. "With one look you can melt a man, and then freeze his heart."

"Oh, that's so romantic," Mary Bubnik cried, as the girls glared back at Miss Gretzky in their best attempt at an icy stare.

Their teacher circled, nodding her head in approval. "Very, very good. I see the ice — now show me the fire."

Gwen, who was very nearsighted without her glasses, blinked blindly in Miss Gretzky's direction. "How?"

"Give me just the tiniest smile," she replied. "One so small that the corners of your mouth barely turn up, and one eyebrow arches like a question mark."

Rocky and McGee faced each other with their fiery half-smiles and raised brows. Then Miss Gretzky called, "Toss your long hair like it's the mane of a beautiful horse."

Mary Bubnik caught Zan doing her fire-and-ice smile and cooed, "Zan, you look beautiful."

"Truly?" Zan asked, dropping her pose.

"Of course," Miss Gretzky agreed. "You are a goddess."

Zan tilted her chin up again and stood tall. For the first time in her life, she *did* feel beautiful and wild. Their compliments made her feel bolder and she did an extra flip of her hair.

"The next time I see Teague McBride," Gwen declared, "I'm going to use my fire-and-ice look on him."

"Oh, no, you don't," McGee objected. "I'm using mine."

"Well, I'm sure yours is very different from mine," Gwen said, flipping back her short red hair.

"How can you even think of facing Teague again?" Zan asked. "Especially after what happened yesterday?"

Gwen grimaced. "Oops. I forgot about that."

"How could you forget the biggest humiliation of our lives?" Rocky asked.

Before Gwen could reply, Miss Gretzky turned up the volume of the tape recorder. "Now, girls, let's put it all together! Stomp, heel, stomp, stomp."

They all shouted, "Stomp, heel, stomp, stomp!" and followed Miss Gretzky around the stage with reckless abandon. When the music finished, they heard clapping from the far end of the room. It was Mr. Pulzini.

Miss Gretzky suddenly dropped her pose and hurried to find her hair pins. "Oh, hello, Ron. We didn't see you come in."

"You were all too busy dancing up a storm. What kind of dance is that?" he asked.

"Uh, um . . ." Miss Gretzky wrung her hands nervously.

"It's called flamenco," Rocky jumped in. "Miss Gretzky said that if we got our ballet steps right, she'd show us a new kind of dance."

"Well, it's very impressive," Mr. Pulzini remarked. He started to leave, then stuck his head back in the door. "By the way, your hour is up. It's almost lunch-time."

As the girls were leaving, Miss Gretzky patted Rocky lightly on the shoulder. "Thanks for keeping my little secret. I hope I can do the same for you."

Rocky shrugged. "It's no big deal."

Although she sounded casual on the outside, inside Rocky felt very proud that she had been able to help out a new friend.

That afternoon after lunch the girls were given an hour of free time. Gwen decided to write a letter to her parents. She stopped by the front office to buy a postcard and found J.P. behind the cash register.

"I need a postcard," Gwen said as she held out her dime. "Do you have any with pictures of deer, or squirrels? My mom said I should get to know some wildlife."

"We only have one postcard for sale," J.P. said, pointing to a stack of old color postcards. It showed an aerial view of the camp that made it difficult to tell what anything was. "But I think that photograph must've been taken twenty years ago."

Gwen shoved the dime across the counter. "Good, it'll show my parents just how chintzy this camp really is.

"Great!" J.P. nodded her head. "Then maybe they'll make a donation, and we'll get better equipment."

"This place needs more than a donation," Gwen replied. "It needs to win the lottery."

J.P. burst out laughing. "You said it."

Gwen looked at the postcard and shook her head. "How come you stay here if you don't like it?"

"Who said I didn't like it?" J.P. ripped open a pack of chocolate-covered granola bars that she'd pulled from under the counter. "If you ask me, it's a hundred times better than Camp Scotsvale."

"Why do you say that?" Gwen asked, hungrily eyeing the treats in J.P.'s hand.

"Well, those girls have everything and they're still a bunch of jerks." J.P. tore off the plastic covering and automatically handed Gwen one of the granola bars. "We, on the other hand, have nothing and we're . . ." She took a bite of her bar and paused to think. "Well, we're not jerks."

Gwen stood munching thoughtfully. She realized that J.P. was right. So far, all of the girls Gwen had met at Camp Claude Harper were pretty weird, but not one of them was mean or snotty. She was even starting to really like J.P.

"Which is why," J.P. continued, "we've got to give it all we've got in the Sports Face-Off with Camp Scotsvale tomorrow."

"Tomorrow?" Gwen nearly choked on her granola bar. "Nobody told us that. I'm not ready!"

"Don't worry." J.P. hopped up on a stool behind the counter. "It's just your basic running, swimming, jumping, kind of contest."

Gwen pushed her glasses up on her nose. "I don't run, I barely swim, and I *never* jump."

J.P. threw back her head and laughed. "Then you can concentrate on the fun things, like the sack race, the egg toss, and the Tug O' War."

"Fun?" Gwen tried to sound enthusiastic but the thought of competing against the Bunheads in any sort of contest made her nervous. Gwen hurried out of the office, completely forgetting her postcard. She had to warn the gang right away. They only had one day to prepare for another battle with the Bunheads.

Chapter Nine

My Life at Camp
by
Suzannah Reed

Day Four — The Great Sports Face-Off

This day has been truly incredible! The moment the girls from Camp Scotsvale arrived in their silver bus, we knew we were in trouble. Scotsvale won the archery contest, the canoe races, and the soccer match. Even though McGee scored three goals for our side, it wasn't enough. By noon it looked as if we didn't have a chance.

Then suddenly we started winning. The Tug O'War is what turned things around. Some of the girls at Camp Claude Harper are not what you would call slim. In truth, they are pretty fat. So when the whistle blew, Gwen shouted, "Everybody, sit down!" And we won!

Now we're all excited. We just might be able to beat Camp Scotsvale! I have to go now. The afternoon contests are about to start.

Suzannah Reed

Zan closed her journal and tucked it into her Navaho rug bag. Then she hurried over to the lawn by the lodge for the start of the three-legged race.

The rest of the gang was already there, along with Arvid and the Rand sisters. Arvid was wearing baggy plaid shorts that hung nearly to her knees. The Rands were all in matching green tee shirts and shorts, which revealed a family trait Zan had never noticed before. They were all knock-kneed.

"Has everyone got a partner?" Ron Pulzini shouted, running up to join them. "Because you'll need one of these to tie your legs together." He held up some colorful strips of material.

"Me and Rocky are one team," McGee declared.

Mary Bubnik and Gwen reached for a strip together.

Zan smiled at Arvid. "I think we should pair up, because our legs are the longest."

"Now remember," Ron Pulzini said, as the girls readied themselves, "the secret to a three-legged race is not speed, but keeping a steady rhythm."

Arvid raised her hand. "Mr. Pulzini, would it help if we all hummed a tune while we ran?"

Ron Pulzini's face burst into a huge grin. "What a magnificent idea. Now . . ." He scratched his balding head. "We need to think of the perfect tune."

"How about a march?" Rafaella Rand suggested. "Like 'The Stars and Stripes Forever'?"

"But I don't know that," Rocky and Mary Bubnik said at the same time.

Mr. Pulzini pressed his lips together and thought. "It needs to be something each of you know and in four/four time." He caught the gang's puzzled expressions and explained, "That's the march rhythm. You know." He waved his hand in the air like a conductor. "One, two, three, four. One, two, three, four."

Mary Bubnik watched his hand beat out the four counts and she started singing to herself, "Old Macdonald had a farm . . ."

Mr. Pulzini pointed at her. "Excellent choice! And then, as you feel comfortable with your partner, pick up the pace."

Rocky and McGee led their teams over to the starting line. Each team mumbled the nursery song over and over again under their breath, trying to get in step.

Courtney Clay and Page Tuttle were already lined up with the teams from Camp Scotsvale.

"Now I've heard everything," Courtney jeered, as she listened to Rocky and McGee practice their song.

The starter pistol was fired and the air was filled with high voices singing "Old MacDonald" but each at a different tempo. Two by two, the entrants hobbled down the field. Gwen and Mary Bubnik promptly got in an argument over whether the farmer had a dog first, or a pig. That slowed them down a lot.

But McGee and Rocky charged out, singing as fast as they could. "With a quack-quack here, and a quack-quack there!" At the mulberry tree, they passed a startled Courtney and Page and headed for home. They crossed the chalked line with a final chorus of "Eee-yie, eee-yie, *oh!*"

Mary Bubnik and Gwen stopped arguing and started screaming, "We won, we won!"

The mood had changed. With the score at 3–2, and only two events remaining, the Scotsvale girls were starting to feel a little less confident. The Claude Harper girls were smiling and laughing as they gathered at the edge of the driveway for the baseball toss.

Scotsvale jumped to a quick lead with a hefty throw by a girl named Janis. Rocky's toss came within a few feet but no one else even came close. Finally there were only two girls left to throw for Claude Harper.

Gwen was one of them. She grabbed the ball and, with a mighty "Arrgh!", hurled it as hard as she could. It flew about five yards and dropped to the ground.

Hoots of laughter erupted from the Scotsvale rooters.

But Gwen wasn't upset. She knew her team had a secret weapon — Katie McGee, who was an all-star catcher in Little League. She could throw a ball to second base faster than any boy could in Fairview, Ohio.

"Okay, McGee," Gwen said, as she flipped the baseball into her friend's hand. "Give it all you got!"

McGee grinned as she took her place at the edge of the driveway. She stared at the narrow strip of grass that ran along the strip in front of their tents. She thought of her Little League baseball diamond in Fairview and imagined she was trying to hit the scoreboard in centerfield. McGee took a deep breath and, drawing back her arm, let it fly.

The ball arched up over the grass and Trudy Pulzini's herb garden. It soared past the big green Dumpster and over the tents. Then there was a giant intake of breath from the crowd as the little white ball sailed out of sight into the woods.

"Home run!" Rocky declared.

J.P. grabbed McGee by the arm and raised it above

her head. "The winner!" she shouted with glee.

"Yeow!" McGee clutched her shoulder and fell to the ground in pain.

The counselors were at her side in a flash. "Are you all right?" Marge Ledbetter asked, her eyes dark with concern.

McGee poked at her shoulder and winced. "I think I pulled something."

"Is she going to be all right?" Ron Pulzini asked, as he and Trudy joined the little group.

"Looks like she's wrenched her shoulder," Harry Hackerwood replied. "She needs to keep it still for a while."

"Take her into the lodge, and we'll put a cold pack on it," Marge Ledbetter ordered. "We don't want it to swell up."

"Right." Harry scooped McGee up in his arms and carried her into the lodge.

"Ice!" Marge Ledbetter barked at some Scotsvale girls lounging by a cooler. "Bring the ice — now!"

The rest of the gang stood dumbfounded as they watched the little procession take McGee away.

"This is a disaster," J.P. moaned. "Now we're sunk."

The last event was the obstacle course and each camp had picked their best athlete to run it. McGee had been the logical choice to represent Camp Claude Harper.

"Does this mean we lose?" Mary Bubnik asked.

84

"Of course," Gwen snapped peevishly. "We don't have a ghost of a chance."

"Says who?" Rocky protested. "We can't just give up now. Not when we're so close to beating those Bunheads." Rocky glared at the little band of girls and declared, "They may be better athletes, but we've got something they don't have."

"What?" Zan asked quietly.

"Heart." Rocky slammed her palm against her chest. "My dad always says that heart is more important than anything else."

"But, Rocky, it's the obstacle course," J.P. pointed out.

"So?"

"We call it The Killer," Rowena Rand muttered. "In the three years that I've been coming here, I've never been able to get around it even once."

"And we've just lost our best athlete," J.P. pointed out.

"So we get someone else," Rocky said. "Right?"

A tiny smile crossed Zan's face. "I nominate Rocky."

"I second it," J.P. said instantly.

"Me?" Rocky turned pale.

"You and McGee are our best athletes," J.P. said. "If it hadn't been for you two, we never would have aced the three-legged race."

"But I've never even *seen* the obstacle course," Rocky protested.

"Don't worry," Gwen reassured her. "I'll bet you've watched your dad do that stuff a lot."

"Well, yeah," Rocky replied, "but this is kind of different. . . ."

"It's for McGee," Mary Bubnik cut in urgently.

"And the camp," J.P. added.

"And for all of us," Zan finished.

Suddenly, the loudspeaker crackled and Ron Pulzini's voice announced, "The final event of the day — the obstacle course — is about to begin. The course consists of the tire maze, scaling the wall, the belly crawl, a wind sprint, and finishing off with a — "

There was a wail of feedback and then the loudspeaker sputtered and went dead.

"What was that last part?" Rocky asked Gwen.

Gwen shook her head. "I don't know. The speaker conked out."

Suddenly the speaker blared on more loudly than ever. "Testing, testing, one, two, three," Ron Pulzini's voice blasted out at earsplitting volume and everyone covered their ears in pain. "Um, is this working?"

Shouts of "Yes!" echoed from all over the camp.

"Then will the obstacle course contestants please take their marks at the starting line? And may the best camp win!"

Rocky was in shock. Without thinking, she let the others guide her over to the starting line. As they walked along, other girls from their camp patted her on the shoulder and wished her good luck. She began to feel her confidence return.

It can't be that hard, Rocky thought to herself. I'm tougher than most of the boys I know. How's some girl from Snotsvale going to stop me?

Marge Ledbetter hurried up to Rocky as she was lacing up her sneakers. "Okay, now the important thing in an event like this is to stay calm."

The counselor was anything but calm. Her hands fluttered nervously and she giggled between words. "For the first time in ten years, our camp has a real chance to win the Face-Off." She giggled again, and then tried to regain her composure. "I don't want to put any pressure on you, but *everything* is resting on this race." She paused, then said in a husky voice, "I just want you to know that I am very, *very* proud to be your counselor and coach."

For one second Rocky thought Marge the Sarge was going to cry.

"One last piece of advice," Marge Ledbetter added. *"Relax!"*

She bellowed the word so loudly that Rocky nearly fell backwards. Then Rowena Rand raised her trumpet to her lips and bugled the cavalry call. "Charge!"

The Scotsvale girl was already in position. She was immense — at least a head taller than Rocky. Her full-body running suit had neon stripes down the legs, and she wore heavy knee and elbow pads. On her headband was printed the name "Moose."

Rocky held out her hand and said, "Good luck."

The girl just stared at her. "Eat my dust, clod-hopper."

Rocky was about to deliver a stinging retort when the starter shouted, "Ladies, take your marks."

She knelt down in a sprinter's crouch and, when the pistol went off, lunged toward the tire maze.

"Raise your knees high!" voices shouted from the sidelines.

Rocky didn't need to be reminded. She'd seen her brothers run this exercise a thousand times in football practice. She glanced over at the Scotsvale girl and grinned. The girl was strong but Rocky was faster. She finished the run a full two seconds ahead.

"Go, go, go!" Gwen, Zan, and Mary Bubnik chanted from the sidelines.

Rocky dug her head down and sprinted for the rope climb, which was a tall wooden wall with two ropes dangling down the front of it. Rocky leaped onto a rope and tried pulling herself hand over hand up the wall. But she didn't have enough strength in her arms.

"Use your legs!" Marge Ledbetter shouted from the sidelines. "Keep yourself parallel to the ground and walk up."

Rocky bit her lip and clambered up the wooden planking. Just as she neared the top, three taunting voices sang out, "Garcia, your rope is slipping!"

Rocky looked up, startled, and nearly fell.

Marge Ledbetter was furious. "You! With the buns on your heads! Put a cork in it!"

Rocky saw Courtney, Page, and Alice cower backwards and a smile crossed her lips. She regained her footing, scampered over the top, and jumped to the ground. Then she turned her full attention to what lay ahead.

A long, narrow tarp had been stretched across the next twenty yards, making a tunnel. Rocky threw herself onto her belly and, diving under it, pulled herself along on her elbows straight to the end. She wondered if Marge the Sarge had designed this part of the contest. It looked suspiciously like something from boot camp.

"Way to go, Rocky," Gwen shouted, as she burst out from under the tarp into the sunlight. "You're a full event ahead of the Moose."

Rocky threw back her head and laughed. Her elbows were skinned and she had a rope burn on her right hand but she wasn't winded at all. In fact, she felt exhilarated as she sprinted through the woods.

Girls from both camps lined the path. As she whizzed by the cheering crowd, she glimpsed J.P. and Mr. and Mrs. Pulzini, grinning and waving. Then all the faces blurred as she kicked into overdrive and flew toward the final obstacle.

The course opened out into the meadow by the lake and in the distance Rocky could see a big red numeral four posted on the dock.

"The last event must be a rowing contest," she thought to herself. She looked over her shoulder and watched the girl from Scotsvale lumber out of the woods. "If I get there before the Moose, I've won."

Mary Bubnik and Zan had positioned themselves

by the red numeral and, as Rocky pounded by them, cheered, "You did it, Rocky! We're going to win. You did it!"

Rocky hopped onto the dock and ran to the end of the pier, then suddenly screeched to a halt. She spun in a circle, jogging in place.

"Where's the boat?" she shouted toward the judges, who were now lined up on the shore.

"There is no boat," Marge Ledbetter called as she raced down to the shore line. "You just have to swim to the buoy, and back." She cupped her hands around her mouth and ordered, "Dive, Rocky, dive!"

But Rocky couldn't move. She stared down at the dark murky water in a panic. "Oh, no," she moaned, "oh, *no!*"

By this time the rest of the crowd had caught up and were screaming, "Rocky, dive! *Dive!*"

From off in the field, two faint voices could be heard, screaming, "No! Don't!"

But Arvid and Miss Gretzky were drowned out as the Scotsvale girls started chanting, "Moose! Moose! Moose!"

Rocky stood paralyzed at the end of the dock. Behind her she could hear the big girl's feet pound down the wooden planks. Then a loud splash followed, a roar went up from the crowd, and her heart sank.

"Rocky, what's the matter?" a familiar voice shouted from behind her. Rocky turned around to see McGee hurrying toward her, her right arm in a sling.

"Come on, Rocky," McGee urged. "Don't choke!"

Rocky felt hot tears burn her eyes. She had two choices. She could confess on the spot, and be totally humiliated in front of her friends and everybody from both camps, or she could jump in the water, and never be seen again.

Rocky looked up at the mass of people and suddenly grew dizzy. She stepped back and fell right off the pier into the water.

As she went under, the roar of the crowd disappeared. Rocky had expected to just keep going down and down into the bottomless lake but things didn't work out that way. Her feet hit something hard and she jolted to a halt.

She straightened her knees and suddenly her head was back above water. With a jolt, Rocky realized the water came barely above her waist. She turned, ready to make a run for the buoy. But it was too late.

Moose had already tagged up and was churning through the water like a tugboat for the finish. As the crowd rushed down the dock to congratulate the winner, Rocky thought to herself, That's it. My life is over.

Chapter Ten

Dinner that evening was gloomy for the girls from Claude Harper. There was none of the usual horsing around between tables. Everyone ate their meal in silence. And no one complained about the food, not even Gwen.

Ron Pulzini tried to cheer them up with a couple of corny jokes but no one had the heart to laugh. That was because they all knew the worst was yet to come after dinner.

"I don't know why we have to go to a stupid bonfire with those jerks from Snotsvale," McGee complained as she and the gang walked up the path to the campfire area.

"Another year of having to sit and listen to them

brag about how great they are," J.P. said as she joined the gang.

"It's truly awful," Zan said with a shake of her head. "I don't think I can bear it."

"Face the facts, guys," Gwen muttered. "We really are a bunch of clodhoppers."

"I don't know why y'all are so depressed," Mary Bubnik said. "After all, my mother always says, winning isn't everything."

"No," Rocky mumbled. "It's the only thing."

Rocky felt as though she'd let everyone down. The worst part was that no one had blamed her for losing the Sports Face-Off. In fact, no one had said a thing about it. She would've felt better if they had.

The bonfire was blazing brightly when they reached the circle of log benches around the fire pit. The girls from Camp Scotsvale had taken over half of the benches and were laughing and giggling merrily together.

In the very center Courtney Clay was holding court, with Page and Alice on each side. Her eyes sparkled with a triumphant gleam as she saw the gang from Camp Claude Harper slouch toward a row of empty seats near the back.

One Scotsvale girl had a guitar and was leading the others in a rousing rendition of "The Happy Wanderer."

"Val da-ree, val-da-rah, val-da-ree," they sang.

Then Courtney turned toward the gang and sang

mockingly, "Val-da-ra-HA-HA-HA-HA-HA!"

This cracked up the Bunheads so much they had to stop singing.

"Watch out for that puddle, Garcia," Alice Wescott called as Rocky moved to her bench. "You forgot your water wings."

Rocky tried to ignore her crack but all around she could hear people whispering, "That's the girl who couldn't swim!"

"Let's have a big cheer for the losers," Courtney declared, standing up and gesturing to her friends.

"Two, four, six eight, who do we appreciate?" the Scotsvale girls shouted. "Camp Clodhopper!"

As the cheer disintegrated into gales of mocking laughter, the girls from Claude Harper stared glumly at the ground.

Then the counselors from both camps came in, led by Marge Ledbetter. She walked stiffly to the far edge of the campfire ground, turned and stood with her hands behind her back, and stared straight ahead. Rocky decided she looked just like one of the sentries who was always posted at the gate to the Air Force base.

Mr. Pulzini cleared his throat noisily. "I'd, um, just like to congratulate our friends from across the lake."

There was loud applause from the Scotsvale girls as their director, a gray-haired woman dressed in a crisp white dress, got up next. "Thank you, Ron," the woman said in a thin, nasal voice. "As always, it's been a pleasure for us to share another day of fine sportsmanship and friendly competiton."

"She sounds like she's got a plug up her nose," Gwen remarked, which made the others giggle.

The woman caught their laughter and narrowed her eyes slightly. Then a thin smile crossed her lips. "Perhaps some day your girls will be the ones giving the victory cheer. After all, there's always next year. . . ."

"Not if I have anything to say about it," J.P. muttered.

Ron Pulzini gave his daughter a stern look and then turned to Harry Hackerwood, who was sitting quietly in an old canvas camp chair, clutching a tin cup of coffee. "Now, tonight Harry will share with us what we at Camp Claude Harper like to call The Legend."

Harry raised his eyes from his cup and looked at all the faces seated around the campfire. Then he began. "Tonight's sad tale concerns three girls who came to this camp ten years ago." He glanced up at the dark sky and added in a low tone, "It was on a night much like this one — moonless, cloudless — that they met Ol' Griz."

"Ol' Griz?" McGee repeated. "Who's that?"

Harry lifted his cup to his lips and took a deep sip of coffee. "Only the biggest, meanest grizzly that ever came marauding down from Alaska."

"Wait a minute," Courtney protested. "There aren't any grizzly bears in Ohio."

Harry shrugged. "Try telling that to his victims."

He paused and added, "If you can find anything left of them."

"You're kidding," Page Tuttle exclaimed. Harry stared at her without blinking. She gulped and added, "Aren't you?"

"Once I thought I caught sight of Ol' Griz disappearing into a cave on Wild Horse Island," Ron Pulzini said.

"Other people say he lives at the bottom of Lake Charles," Marge Ledbetter whispered.

Harry nodded. "One thing we do know — Ol' Griz never gets hungry until the dark of the moon. Then he can be heard searching the woods, like some beast from a nightmare."

The Rand sisters, who were sitting on one of the log benches, huddled tightly together.

"I hear his teeth are as sharp as knives, and his claws are almost a foot long. On moonless nights he suddenly appears and — *whoosh!*" Harry swept the air with his arm and the girl closest to him let out a tiny shriek. "He's got you!"

Mary Bubnik shivered and clutched Zan's hand. Gwen zipped up her sweatshirt and pulled the hood over her head. "I've always hated bears," she announced to no one in particular. "Even teddy bears."

"I thought it was bugs," McGee whispered.

Gwen pushed her glasses firmly up onto her nose with one finger. "I have a *long* hate list." Then to emphasize her point, she glared at the Bunheads.

"So what happened to the three girls?" Zan asked timidly.

"These three girls had been warned never to leave camp alone," Harry continued in a low voice, "but they wouldn't listen. And so one moonless night, they took a flashlight and hiked out into the darkness."

J.P. leaned forward. "I heard they were going to spend the night on Wild Horse Island."

Harry nodded. "That may have been their destination, but they never reached it."

Mary Bubnik inhaled sharply. "Did Ol' Griz get them?"

"No one really knows for sure. The people back at camp heard a terrible roar that echoed across the lake, followed by a single piercing scream. Then there was a loud splash, as if some incredibly huge creature had dived into the lake. And then all was still."

No one spoke for a moment. Finally, Rowena Rand asked in a shaky voice, "Did they ever find the three girls?"

"A search party found their canoe, crushed against the rocks of Desperation Point — but there was no sign of those girls. It was as if they'd completely vanished from the face of the earth."

"Maybe they just ran away," Courtney whispered.

Harry shrugged. "Maybe. But how would you explain the voices?"

"What voices?" Page Tuttle asked.

"The ones that come drifting across the lake, crying — " He made his voice sound far, far away. "H-e-e-e-l-p meeee! I'm lo-o-o-o-o-st!"

Harry tossed a rock into the fire and several embers exploded with a loud snap. Everyone jerked back in alarm, and a few girls tittered nervously at their jumpiness.

"Whether Ol' Griz got them, we'll never know," Harry said. "But their ghosts seem doomed to wander these dark hills forever, searching for their way home."

He poured the last few drops of his coffee into the fire. As the coals sizzled and steamed, he looked up at the silent ring of girls. "That's it for tonight's tale. Sleep well, everyone," He wiggled his eyebrows ghoulishly. "And remember, don't leave camp alone!"

No one moved a muscle. Finally, Ron Pulzini stood up. "Thank you, Harry. And thank you, Camp Scotsvale, for joining us."

The director of Camp Scotsvale rose to her feet and her girls did the same.

Ron Pulzini turned to a short Asian girl sitting next to him. "And now, Ginee Seo will finish this day with a song. Ginee?"

The slender girl smiled shyly and rose to her feet. She opened her mouth and sang in a high, clear voice, "Day is done, gone the sun, from the sky."

"That's 'Taps,' " Rocky whispered to McGee. "On

the Air Force base, a bugler plays that in the barracks."

"All is well, safely rest, day is done." Ginee bowed her head.

The girls from Scotsvale left in their silver camp bus and then the counselors from Camp Claude Harper walked the girls back to their tents.

"I won't sleep a wink tonight," Gwen said flatly. "Not after that story."

"Don't worry," J.P. reassured her. "Ol' Griz hasn't been seen around here in years."

"I'm not worried about him," Gwen said as the gang arrived at their tent. "I'm worried about those three lost ghosts. What if they finally find our camp — and they want to stay in *our* tent?"

Chapter Eleven

Once the gang had changed into their nightgowns and settled snugly into their beds, Marge Ledbetter appeared at the tent flap.

"All right, campers," she barked. "I'll be patrolling the grounds this evening, making sure your lights are out, and your lips are sealed. Get it?"

"Got it!" the gang shouted back.

"Good." As the camp counselor walked away, they heard her call, "I'll see you at sunrise."

"Sunrise?" Gwen groaned.

"Boy, we'd better sleep fast," Mary Bubnik drawled, "or we'll be too tired to do anything tomorrow."

"Sleep fast?" Zan asked, as she made sure her journal was safely tucked away under her pillow. "How do you do that?"

"Well, you skip dreaming, and go immediately into deep sleep," Mary replied, tugging her covers up over her shoulders.

Rocky raised up on one elbow. "Mary Bubnik, did anyone ever tell you you're weird?"

Mary cocked her head in thought. "Why, yes, several people have," she replied. "But I tell them I'm not weird, I'm just different."

Rocky flopped her head back onto her pillow and smiled. Mary Bubnik was definitely different, but Rocky liked her that way.

Gwen yawned loudly and punched her pillow with her fist. "Four down, six to go."

"Six what?" Zan asked.

"Six days till we leave this place. I can't wait." Gwen rolled over onto her stomach. "Good night, everybody."

"'Night," McGee answered sleepily. "Try not to think about Ol' Griz and the three ghosts."

"You had to say that, didn't you?" Gwen complained. "Now I'm going to skip the dreams, and go straight to the nightmares."

"Birch Patrol!" a voice bellowed from off in the distance. "Put a cork in it — this minute."

"Wow!" Mary Bubnik whispered. "She must have supersonic hearing."

"I do!" the voice answered back. "And that's one demerit for your tent."

"Oh, great," Gwen groaned. "We're never going to be first in line to eat."

"That's two demerits."

There was an anguished moan from the gang, but no one said another word. Pretty soon, they all lay quietly, snoozing in their beds. Far off in the distance, Beethoven, the Pulzinis' basset hound, could be heard baying in the woods. Soon the only sound in the calm air was the lulling chirp of crickets.

Suddenly McGee bolted upright. She leaned across and tapped Rocky on the shoulder. "Rocky! Are you awake?"

Rocky groaned and rolled over. "I am now. What is it?"

"I thought I heard something."

"Like what?"

"It sounded like tinfoil being squished together."

"Now what would ghosts be doing with tinfoil?" Rocky mumbled.

"I don't know," McGee said, "but there it goes again." The girls froze, cocking their heads to hear better in the darkness. The next thing they heard was a loud crunch.

"Now it sounds like chewing," Rocky said.

"Yeah," McGee added, "and I smell peanuts."

"There's only one person I know of who makes that sound." Rocky flicked on her flashlight and the beam caught Gwen in mid-bite.

"Gwendolyn Hays!" McGee gasped. "What are you doing eating a Snickers bar? Don't you know we're not supposed to have candy in our tent?"

"I'm hungry," Gwen mumbled with her mouth full.

"How much candy have you got in here?" Rocky hopped out of her cot and padded barefoot across the wooden floor.

Gwen stopped chewing and retreated down beneath her covers. "Not much. Brownie ate all my trail mix, so I only have a few snacks left."

"Come on, Gwen," McGee hissed, joining Rocky. " 'Fess up."

Rocky shone her flashlight under Gwen's bed. The light revealed Gwen's heavy leather suitcase and a black-and-orange athletic bag she had borrowed from her brother. As Rocky pulled out the bag, Gwen lunged for it and yelled, "Don't touch that!"

"Too late," Rocky said, opening the bag. She shone her light inside, and trained the beam on Gwen's face. "You call that a few snacks?"

Gwen squinted at the harsh light and put her hand in front of her eyes. "It's hardly enough to last me the rest of the week."

"Look at this," Rocky declared, turning the bag upside down and dumping it on Gwen's mattress. "Twinkies, Ho-Hos, four different kinds of candy bars, sacks of M&Ms, rolls of Lifesavers..." She looked at Gwen in amazement. "For a normal person this would last a lifetime."

McGee joined Rocky at the bed with her own flashlight. "Geez Louise, Gwen, you could open a candy store with that much loot."

103

"You're just upset because I didn't offer you any," Gwen retorted. "Here, have an M&M." She held out a new bag of candy.

"Gwen," McGee scolded. "I really don't think you should have that stuff in the tent. You know what they said about sweets attracting wild animals."

"Wild animals — that's a laugh." Gwen popped an entire handful of M&Ms in her mouth. "The wildest animal we're going to see here at Camp Clodhopper is that frog you threw in the Bunheads' canoe."

Suddenly, a branch cracked loudly in the woods, followed by a heavy thud. The three girls sat paralyzed as a deep rumbling growl sounded from just outside their tent.

"When was the last time you heard a frog growl?" Rocky asked, not moving a muscle.

"Frogs don't growl," McGee replied. "Only dogs and — "

Another ferocious growl roared at them, this time from right under their tent.

M&Ms shot out of Gwen's mouth as she sputtered, "And b-b-b-b-b-b — "

They all screamed, "Bears!"

"It's Ol' Griz," Rocky shouted. "He's under the tent!"

"Give him the food!" McGee grabbed a handful of Twinkies and Ho-Ho's from Gwen's bed and heaved them out their tent flap. Then she grabbed

Gwen's bag and hurled it as far as she could toward the woods.

"Get up!" Rocky cried, throwing back the covers on Mary Bubnik's and Zan's beds. "We're being attacked."

"By what?" Zan asked sleepily.

"Bears!" Gwen choked as several more loud thunks echoed beneath the tent's platform, followed by a ferocious growl.

Mary Bubnik leapt to her feet and stood on top of her bed. "He could reach his big old paw right through the floor and grab us. What do we do?"

"Get out of here!" McGee shrieked.

All five girls bolted for the tent opening at once. They collided in the doorway and the tent pulled off its pegs, collapsing around them.

"He's got me!" Gwen shrieked. She punched wildly at the canvas around her.

"Ouch!" McGee yelled. "Quit hitting me."

Rocky found the tent flap and the five girls exploded out into the cold night air. Gwen ran in a circle in the dark, screaming, "It's Ol' Griz, come to get us!"

"Ol' Griz?" startled voices cried from the other tents. "Let's get out of here!"

The entire Rand family raced out of their tent, clutching their musical instruments to their chests. Arvid bellowed from inside her tent, "Don't come near me, I've got a knife!"

Gwen, with her arms flailing wildly out to the sides, ran headlong through the camp, crashing into bewildered campers, knocking over garbage cans, and trampling flowers.

With her friends struggling to keep up with her, Gwen bolted into Marge Ledbetter's tent. Unfortunately, the commotion had already awakened the counselor and she was bent over, looking for her flashlight when Gwen made contact.

"Ooomph!"

The two tumbled onto Marge Ledbetter's bed, which collapsed with a loud crack. Gwen felt the counselor's fuzzy robe and, thinking it was the bear, screamed, "Oh, my God, he's eaten ol' Leadbottom!"

"Gwen!" Zan and Mary Bubnik shouted from outside the tent. "Run for your life!"

Gwen burst out of Marge Ledbetter's tent in a blind panic and crashed right into McGee, who shrieked, "No! Run for the lodge!"

"Don't!" Rocky caught hold of McGee's nightshirt and it ripped up the back. "A bear can outrun you."

They grabbed hold of each other and jumped up and down, screaming, "What'll we do? What'll we do?"

"Play dead." Rocky threw herself flat on her face on the ground.

McGee, Zan, and Mary Bubnik followed suit immediately. Gwen was still running in a circle, shrieking, "We're being eaten by a bear!"

Big spotlights popped on from tall poles around the lodge and more girls took up the cry of, "Bear in camp!"

This just confirmed Gwen's fears and she yelled even louder. Rocky finally managed to grab Gwen by the ankle and yanked her foot out from under her. Gwen hit the ground with a loud wail.

"Ol' Griz has got me!" she howled. "I'm gonna die, I'm gonna — *mrrmph!*"

Rocky threw her arm over Gwen's head and smothered her cries. The five girls lay shaking with fear, their faces buried in the dirt.

McGee's heart was pounding so loudly that she barely heard the footsteps padding up to them. She held her breath and prepared for the worst.

Then a familiar voice whispered above their heads, "Ha, ha, the joke's on you!"

Chapter Twelve

Dear Diary,

Boy, things are sure exciting around here! Last night the Bunheads pretended to be Ol' Griz and scared us so bad we wrecked our tent. Then Gwen knocked down the camp's clothesline and ruined Mrs. Pulzini's garden. Then Miss Ledbetter came out of her tent with funny cream all over her face and gave us the most demerits ever recorded at camp — TEN. Eight were for wrecking the camp and two were for laughing at her. But she sure looked funny. Now we have to clean the yucky old latrines.

Your friend, Mary

When Mary reached the little outhouses lined up behind the lodge, McGee was already distributing mops and buckets to the rest of the gang. Then she passed around several blue-and-red bandannas.

"What're these for?" Zan asked.

"To put over your nose," McGee explained. She folded hers into a triangle and tied it around her head. "Now here's the plan." She held up a bucket full of sudsy water. "First, one of us throws open the door, then runs into the outhouse and sloshes Mr. Clean onto the floor." She held up a mop and said, "The next person goes in and spreads it around." She pointed to a bucket full of clear water. "Then someone does the rinse cycle, and we're done. That way, nobody has to suffer very long."

"Good plan," Rocky said approvingly.

"Speaking of suffering," Gwen said, as she tightened her scarf, "why do we always have to be the last to eat at every meal?"

"Because we always have the most demerits," Mary Bubnik pointed out.

"But we've been here five days and so far we've had to wash the dishes twice, take out the garbage three times, and now we're cleaning these awful latrines," Gwen finished.

"It's all the Bunheads' fault," Rocky declared. She threw open the outhouse door, flipped up the toilet seats, and sloshed a bucket of sudsy water around the room. "First they humiliate us in the trail ride. Then they destroy us in the Sports Face-Off. And *last* night they tried to scare us to death."

"Tried to?" Zan repeated, taking the mop from McGee. "I'd say they succeeded." She took a deep breath, ducked inside, and spread the suds around the floor.

"I wasn't scared," Rocky said. She rinsed her mop in the bucket of clean water. "I knew a real bear wouldn't crawl under our tent."

"Then why did you make us bury our faces in the dirt?" Mary Bubnik demanded.

"Yeah," McGee said, putting her hands on her hips. "And why did you rip the back of my brand-new nightshirt?"

"And mutilate my *entire* supply of Twinkies?" Gwen cried, yanking the mop out of Rocky's hands.

"Don't shout at me," Rocky snapped. "You're the one who single-handedly destroyed the entire camp. Now we're going to spend the rest of our time here cleaning latrines."

"Is this a private fight, or can anybody join in?" a voice asked from behind them.

When Rocky turned around, she found herself looking into the bluest eyes she'd ever seen. "It's ... it's ..." Rocky stammered. *"Him."*

"Who?" Gwen spun around so fast she rapped herself in the forehead with the mop handle. The blow made her stagger backwards into the stall.

"Look out, Gwen," McGee cried. "You're going to fall in the — "

But the warning came too late. Gwen fell right into

one of the open toilet seats, where she lodged tight as a drum.

"Get me out of here!" she wailed, flailing her limbs helplessly like a beetle on its back.

Rocky and McGee grabbed her by the arms and popped her loose. Gwen rushed outside and headed directly for her dance bag that lay on the ground.

"Gross, gross, gross," she muttered as she jerked her can of Buzz Off out of her dance bag and covered herself with the thick mist.

"Gwen!" Rocky coughed and waved her hand in front of her face. "What are you doing?"

"Some ugly spider might have jumped on me while I was stuck in there," Gwen said, still spraying.

"So what are you trying to do, drown him?" McGee asked, slipping her bandanna back over her face.

"I'm not taking any chances." Gwen stopped spraying herself and aimed the can at the air and ground around her. "I want to make sure he's dead."

"If you don't stop spraying that stuff right now, we're all going to collapse." Rocky grabbed hold of Gwen's arm and yanked the can out of her hand.

Gwen swatted at herself a few more times just to be on the safe side. Then she looked up at Teague McBride and said accusingly, "You scared me."

"Sorry about that." The wrangler pushed his cowboy hat back on his head. "Are you all right?"

Teague was standing with J.P., Arvid Epstein, and all four Rand sisters. They were carrying cans of paint, brushes, and rolls of poster board. The Rands also had their instruments strapped to their backs.

"What's going on?" McGee asked.

"J.P. told me about the dirty trick the Scotsvale girls played on you last night," Teague explained. "I thought you might want a chance to get back at them."

"You're on our side?" Mary Bubnik asked, wide-eyed.

"Sure. I just work for Camp Scotsvale, I don't hang around with them." Teague grinned at J.P., who stepped forward.

"Teague and I are best friends," she explained. "We go to the same school in town."

"Off-season those girls wouldn't even know I was alive," Teague said with a shake of his head. "But because I'm the wrangler at camp they think I'm special."

Zan and the others didn't mention that being cute might have something to do with it, too.

"This morning after breakfast," Arvid Epstein said, "a bunch of us got together and decided to declare war on Camp Scotsvale."

"I'm all for that," Rocky declared, balling her hand into a fist.

"You see," Arvid continued, "we decided that there's a basic flaw in the traditional way these games have been arranged every year."

"Yeah," McGee grumbled, "this camp always loses."

"Ah!" J.P. raised a finger. "But the reason we always lose is because we're a performing arts camp, not a sports camp."

"Could've fooled me," Gwen mumbled, remembering the morning lap swims and the endless marches around the lodge with Miss Ledbetter.

"They beat us and now—" Rafaella Rand raised her instrument in the air, "it's time we beat them!"

"At what?" Gwen asked.

J.P. smiled smugly. "What we do best."

"What *do* we do best?" Mary Bubnik asked, blinking wide-eyed at the group.

"Play music!" J.P. shouted.

"And dance," Arvid added, pointing at the gang.

J.P. folded her arms across her chest. "So we've decided to challenge them to a *talent* Face-Off."

Arvid nodded her head. "Our talents against theirs."

"But who'll be the judges?" Zan asked sensibly.

"We'll get some impartial people from town," Teague answered. "Mr. Mardorf, the high school principal—"

"And Lily Kay of Lily Kay Kosmetics," J.P. added.

"Heck." Teague took off his hat. "I bet we could even get the mayor."

"I've already talked to Ron," J.P. said, "and he's all for it."

"Everyone in camp is thrilled," Arvid exclaimed.

"And Ron said we could hold the competition on

the old stage by the lake," J.P. continued. "We've always held our 'Music Under the Stars' program there. It'll be perfect."

"Here's the official challenge," Arvid declared, extending a large piece of paper rolled up to look like a scroll. "We'll set the contest for this Saturday. That'll give all of us time to rehearse our pieces."

J.P. faced the gang. "This is war!"

McGee raised her mop and started to chant, "Two, four, six, eight, who will we obliterate?" Everyone joined the cheer. "Snotsvale! Snotsvale! G-e-e-e-e-e-e-e-e-t *Snotsvale!*"

Long after the others had gone, the gang continued cheering, shaking their mops in the air and marching around in a circle.

"This is great!" Rocky exulted. "Once and for all, we'll show those Bunheads who's the best."

"Bunheads?" Gwen said, lowering her mop. "Oh, no."

"What's the matter?" Zan asked.

"I've just thought of something." Gwen sank down onto the grass. "They'll probably do a ballet dance in the talent show."

"So?" Rocky replied.

"So." She looked up at the others and said bluntly, "Let's face it, they're better ballerinas than we are."

"That's right." McGee slumped down beside her. "They'll stomp all over us."

"And then we'll let everyone down again," Rocky said, chewing nervously on her lip.

"Not if we do our own special dance," Zan declared, her eyes suddenly twinkling.

"And what dance is that?" Mary Bubnik asked.

Zan dropped her pail to the ground and did a couple of stomps with her heel.

"Flamenco!"

Chapter Thirteen

Dear Journal,

Okay, I know I should have written sooner but, Geez Louise, a lot has been happening! Tonight is the big talent contest and everyone is a nervous wreck. We had stewed prunes for breakfast and the entire Rand family threw up purple barf. Total gross-out!

Everyone, even Marge the Sarge, has been working hard. She, Rocky, and Arvid are planning a secret act that they'll show us all tonight. I've been working with Teague McBride. He's teaching me to ride Jingles — bareback. Mary Bubnik

116

said she's planning to tell a few jokes. I
hope she's kidding.
Better go. It's almost showtime.
Katie McGee

McGee set her journal in her lap and stared down at the empty stage. She was sitting on one of the folding chairs that had been set up in rows along the sloping hill facing the dock.

Harry Hackerwood, with the help of Rocky, J.P., and the viola section of the orchestra, had built tall cloth panels to act as theater wings, so the audience couldn't see the performers as they waited to come on. Spotlights hung from metal poles at the back of the audience, and the stage itself was decorated with wicker baskets overflowing with wildflowers that Zan and the Rand sisters had gathered that morning.

The roar of an engine made McGee turn her head. A long silver bus was rolling into the parking lot. She shut her journal and sighed. "The Bunheads have arrived."

She slipped out of the audience and hurried toward the lodge. Mrs. Pulzini had promised to do the girls' hair and makeup and McGee didn't want to be late.

Just around the bend and out of sight of the stage, Rocky and Arvid were standing in matching striped tank suits with big fluffy towels wrapped around them. They had just gone through their special number one last time for Marge Ledbetter.

"Girls, you've made me proud," Marge Ledbetter declared, gruffly. "I can't believe how far you've come in the last four days."

"Thank you, sir — I mean, ma'am," Rocky said, "but we still have a long way to go." They had been taking private lessons with Marge Ledbetter. It had been intense and Rocky had learned a lot but she still felt pretty shaky about swimming. "What I mean is, I'm not sure if I'm ready to perform."

"You're ready." Marge Ledbetter dismissed her doubts with a wave of her hand. "Tonight you'll look like real pros. Just remember when you hear the opening music, wade into the water and do exactly what we rehearsed."

Arvid stared out at the lake. As the sun set behind the trees, the water was looking darker and more scary. "Are you sure it's all shallow?"

"Positive. And don't worry, girls." Marge Ledbetter held up a diving mask and snorkel. "I'll be right out there with you, in case you get scared."

Meanwhile, Gwen was having a nervous breakdown back at the tent. "The show starts in less than half an hour and we don't have a costume!" She fell back on her bed and beat her fist against the pillow. "We're going to lose. I just know it!"

"Gwen, please don't do that!" Zan grabbed Gwen by the arm and pulled her to her feet. "You're going to ruin your hair. And Mrs. Pulzini did such a nice job of curling it."

"How can you talk about hair at a time like this?" Gwen complained. But she sat down on her bed and peered into the mirror on Zan's makeup case. Gwen dabbed at the heavy mascara on her eyes. It was already starting to streak a little.

Zan sat behind her and tried to press some wayward strands of hair back into place. "Miss Gretzky said she'd have our outfits ready in time," Zan said calmly, "and I'm sure she meant it."

"Miss Gretzky's said a lot of things," Gwen muttered. She tore open a new bag of candy with her teeth and popped a handful of M&Ms into her mouth. "She said she's a ballet teacher, and she isn't."

"Instead of complaining," Zan said, "I think we should practice the dance."

"We can't," Gwen replied. "Mary Bubnik is going over her jokes with Harry Hackerman." She shook her head in dismay. "I still can't believe she's really going to do that!"

"Well, Mr. Pulzini thought we needed some humor in the program," Zan said, "and Mary Bubnik was the only one who volunteered."

Gwen fell back on the bed. "She's going to humiliate us all."

"Don't worry about it. Arvid and the other girls in the orchestra are truly wonderful musicians," Zan said softly. "We're sure to win just because of them. And when they see our spectacular dance, I think the judges will be very impressed."

"Shocked is more like it." Gwen checked her watch. " 'Cause if we don't get a costume soon, we'll have to dance in our underwear."

"Knock knock!" a voice sang from outside their tent and then Miss Gretzky stuck her head inside. She looked like she hadn't slept in three days.

"Girls, I am so sorry. Trudy and I tried to sew these costumes ourselves but we got into a little trouble." She extended an armful of faded black dresses with different colored ruffles attached to the hems.

"The sewing machine broke down and we didn't have time to sew them on by hand so some of them are stapled together."

"You stapled our costumes together?" Gwen repeated in shock.

"It's not as bad as it sounds." Miss Gretzky set the dresses on McGee's bed. "Just be careful when you sit down. I think some of the pins are still attached." She started to leave, then paused. "Oh, and we didn't have time to iron them but don't worry — the audience will be watching your dancing, not your clothes."

The bell rang from the lodge and she cried, "Oh, dear. The show starts in ten minutes, and I still have to get the Rands into their band uniforms."

She stumbled out of their tent and the girls looked down at the wrinkled dresses in dismay.

"We'd better try them on," Zan murmured.

They hurriedly pulled on their dresses. Zan's was too big and hung on her like a gunny sack. Gwen's pulled tightly across her middle. "This is worse than I thought," Gwen groaned.

McGee rushed into the tent, followed by Mary Bubnik. "The Bunheads are here!"

"So are our costumes," Gwen said flatly. She and Zan stepped into the middle of the tent and spun in a circle. Zan's stapled ruffle immediately came loose and dangled down against her leg.

Mary Bubnik and McGee stared at them in shocked silence. Finally, Mary said, "Well, they're real different. I don't think the Bunheads will have costumes like these."

"Not if they're lucky," Gwen said, trying to lift her arm above her head. The sleeve dug into her pudgy arm and she cried out in pain. "Yeow! This dress is torture."

"You guys ready?" J.P. was standing in the tent opening. She was wearing her father's tuxedo jacket because tonight she was going to be conducting the camp orchestra. "Come on, it's showtime!"

McGee and Mary Bubnik hurriedly changed into their costumes. Zan carried Rocky's outfit on a hanger and the four of them hurried up to the lodge.

Mr. Pulzini was giving a last-minute pep talk. He was surrounded by girls dressed in a wild assortment of band uniforms. The musicians were busily tuning their instruments and the air was filled with squawks and squeaks.

"Okay, kids, here's the lineup." Ron Pulzini read

from a clipboard. "First we do the processional, followed by our musical concert featuring Ginee Seo. Then there will be a brief interlude of fun and laughter."

"That's me," Mary Bubnik giggled. "I'm the brief interlude."

"Remember, Mary," Gwen whispered, "the emphasis is on *brief*." Gwen had a vision of Mary Bubnik telling her dumb jokes for hours, and the thought made her shudder.

Ron Pulzini smiled at the gang and said, "We finish with your dance, and then the judges will make their decision. Let's go."

The girls filed outside and hurried toward the amphitheater. As the gang passed the parking lot, the door of the big silver bus whooshed open.

"Yoo hoo, Camp Clodhopper!" Courtney Clay called. "Break a leg tonight!'

Normally, that expression meant good luck in the theater, but coming from Courtney, the gang knew it was an insult.

McGee opened her mouth to shout something back but she quickly shut it as six girls dressed in dazzling sequined majorette costumes stepped off the bus behind Courtney. They were followed by ten girls in matching white sailor outfits. Then two workmen lifted a huge cardboard cutout of an ocean liner off the top of the bus.

"Well, that's it," Gwen said, throwing her arms in

the air. "They've got terrific sets and costumes. It's all over. We've lost."

Harry Hackerwood, who was hurrying by with his tin cup of coffee clasped in his hand, stopped when he heard her comment.

"Remember," he whispered, "don't judge a book by its cover. A thousand sequins can't make those girls play a clarinet like Arvid or sing like Ginee." He patted Gwen on the shoulder. "Or dance like you. Be confident."

Then Teague McBride sauntered around the side of the lodge. He was dressed in his best western shirt and pants but, instead of his usual cowboy hat, he had black silk top hat on his head. He smiled at the girls, then put his fingers to his lips and whistled.

Mary Bubnik gasped as Jingles trotted up proudly to Teague's side.

"That can't be Jingles," Gwen exclaimed, squinting at the horse in amazement. "He looks like a totally different animal!"

"We've been working on him all afternoon," McGee said, beaming proudly. "Teague let me braid his mane and put little ribbons in it. Then we brushed his coat and polished his hooves. And look!" She pointed to the horse's rump. "We even put glitter on him."

"Jingles," Zan gushed, "you are truly beautiful!"

"Well, our costumes might be a joke, but at least our horse will look good," Gwen said with a sigh.

Teague touched Jingles lightly on the front leg. "Take a bow, Jingles."

The horse extended his front leg and bent forward.

"How did he know to do that?" Mary Bubnik asked.

"Jingles used to ride with the Western Stars," McGee explained. "He's crossed the country, performing for thousands of people. Haven't you, boy?"

McGee scratched the horse behind his ear and Jingles bobbed his head up and down. That made all the girls laugh and Jingles responded with a loud snort of pleasure.

Then Teague gave McGee a boost onto the horse's bare back. McGee clutched the mane and swallowed hard.

"Now remember what I told you," Teague instructed. "Stay loose. And when you stand up, keep your knees relaxed. Jingles will do the rest."

"You're going to stand up?" Mary Bubnik asked in amazement.

McGee bobbed her head nervously. "I think so."

Mary clapped her hands in delight. "This is going to be the best show ever!"

The sun had just slipped behind the hills on the western shore of Lake Charles, turning the sky a beautiful shade of dusty pink as the audience took their seats in the open air.

The lights dimmed and the Rand sisters, wearing red-white-and-blue satin capes, stepped to the top of the hill. Harry Hackerwood, who was manning one of the spotlights up on the poles, directed the brilliant

124

beam right on J.P., who snapped her fingers and cried, "Ah-one, two, ah-one, two, three — hit it!"

There was a flash of light as the sisters lifted their brass instruments to their lips. Sudenly, the air was filled with the rollicking sound of "When the Saints Go Marching In." The audience applauded in delight as Jingles stepped into the spotlight, with McGee standing on his back. Waving merrily, she led the Camp Claude Harper performers down the aisle toward the stage. The show had begun!

Chapter Fourteen

"Why did the chicken cross the playground?" Mary Bubnik asked the audience.

Someone in the back shouted, "Why?"

"To get to the other slide!"

Mary Bubnik slapped her knee and laughed as loudly as anyone in the crowd.

Backstage Gwen groaned and covered her face. "I can't *believe* she told that joke."

Teague, who was acting as master of ceremonies, stepped to the edge of the stage. "And thank you, Mary Bubnik." He tipped his top hat and urged the audience, "Let's have a big hand for the little lady."

Mary bowed at the polite applause and then raced

into the wings. McGee clapped her on the back.

"Way to go, Mary!" McGee said.

"Oh, y'all, I was so nervous!" Mary took a moment to catch her breath. "How'd I do? Was I okay?"

"You knocked 'em dead," Zan replied.

"Well, I did forget the punch line to that one joke." Mary giggled sheepishly. "And I couldn't remember the start of the other one, but I wrote that last joke myself."

"It sounded like it," Courtney Clay sang out from the darkness. She and the Bunheads were busily warming up in the corner. Each girl was dressed in a fluffy pink tutu, with matching satin toe shoes.

"How did they get such nice costumes?" Zan wondered.

"They must have rented them," Gwen muttered. "They can afford it."

The sound of flutes trilled through the air and McGee whispered, "Come look. Rocky and Arvid are going to show us their surprise."

Onstage J.P. was conducting a quartet of girls while Teague announced, "Ladies and gentlemen, let me direct your attention to the beautiful waters of Lake Charles."

Harry shone the spotlight in a wide arc over the lake.

"What is this I see?" Teague asked in amazement. "Why, a pair of mermaids."

"Fat chance," Courtney cracked.

"Yes, it's the beautiful synchronized swimming of Rochelle Garcia and Arvid Epstein."

The spotlight focused on the two girls as they moved smoothly through the water, their arms arched high above their heads. Keeping time to the music, they dipped their arms into the water and swam first the crawl, then the breast stroke, in perfect unison. There was a ripple in the music and they flipped smoothly onto their backs, their arms never hesitating.

"Isn't that lovely, ladies and gentlemen?" Teague called and the audience applauded appreciatively. "Now the girls will swim the difficult crazy-eight formation, followed by an *arabesque* in the water."

Rocky and Arvid wove in and around each other in a complex flutter of moving limbs. Then, to everyone's surprise, they kicked their legs out of the water high behind them.

"I'm truly impressed," Zan said.

"Me, too," Gwen agreed. "I wouldn't go into that lake after dark for a million dollars. Think of all the creepy things crawling around in there."

"No, I'm talking about Rocky," Zan said. "After only four days with Sarge, she's not only swimming, she's doing water ballet."

McGee glanced across at the Bunheads and smiled. They, too, were amazed as they watched Rocky and Arvid go through their paces. For once, Courtney was speechless.

The number ended with the girls lighting sparklers

that had been attached to two buoys. Then they raised their right arms high out of the water.

"The Statue of Liberty," Teague shouted. "A double vision!"

As the applause thundered, Harry cut the spotlight and Arvid and Rocky disappeared from sight.

Moments later they were standing backstage with the gang, wrapped in thick, fleecy towels. Their teeth were chattering together as the other girls swarmed around to congratulate them.

"All right, you two!" McGee crowed.

"That's the best swimming I've ever seen," Mary Bubnik squealed.

Rocky and Arvid exchanged sly glances, then burst into laughter.

"What's so funny?" Gwen asked.

"We didn't swim," Arvid whispered.

"You didn't?" Mary Bubnik gasped.

Rocky shook her head and whispered, "Arvid and I were just pretending to swim."

"But how?"

"We just walked in the shallow end and moved our arms like we were swimming."

"That is truly amazing," Zan exclaimed. "I never would have guessed."

Gwen pointed to the Bunheads in their corner. "Neither would they. You really wowed 'em."

Rocky beamed with pride. She was no longer afraid of the water and had already decided that as soon as she got back home, she was going to have her dad sign her up for more swimming lessons, brothers or no brothers!

J.P. hurried into the wings. Her face was flushed and she was grinning from ear to ear. "Well, here's the score so far. We've wiped them out in the music department. Your swimming routine sewed up the specialty acts."

Rocky gave Arvid a high five. "All right!"

"And now..." J.P. clapped her hands together and faced the entire gang. "It's up to you guys."

"What do you mean, it's up to us?" Gwen protested.

"If you beat them in the dance section, it'll be a clean sweep for our camp." She patted them on the back. "Go get 'em. I'm going to watch from out front."

Courtney heard their last exchange and trilled, "Too bad you're going to lose the dance contest."

Rocky dropped her towel to the floor. "I say we knock their buns off, right now."

"No, Rocky," Mary Bubnik pleaded. "We're too close to winning."

"You're close, all right," Page said, raising up on her toe shoes. "Second place."

"That's it." Rocky turned to McGee. "Let's get 'em."

She started to charge forward but Gwen grabbed her arm and hissed, "Wait a minute. Did you hear that?"

"Hear what?" Zan whispered.

"That growling sound," Gwen said, swallowing hard.

"Oh, come off it," Rocky said. "That wasn't a growl."

"Wait." Gwen put her finger on her lips. "There it is again. Don't you hear it?"

Everyone backstage cocked their head to listen. This time they heard a low moan, followed by a loud snort.

"That's not funny," Courtney said, backing nervously toward the stage.

"Courtney," Page hissed, "they're trying to scare us like we did them. Don't fall for it."

"Don't worry, I'm not." Courtney folded her arms across her chest and tried to look confident. But even in the half-light the gang could see how wide her eyes were.

"Help me!" a husky voice called.

The gang instantly moved into a tight knot. McGee reached for the hammer that lay on a table backstage.

"I definitely heard that," Zan declared.

Courtney and Alice had gone totally white.

"They have their friends out there, trying to make us blow our ballet." Page raised her voice defiantly. "Well, it won't work. See?"

She marched over to the side of the wall and whispered, "I know you're out there."

Suddenly, a hand reached out of the darkness and grabbed her. There was another low moan and a loud "Sploosh!"

"Aiiieeee!" Page squealed at the top of her lungs

as a huge furry head rammed her in the stomach. She ran past the gang, past Courtney and Alice, and right onto the stage just as the taped music for "Waltz of the Flowers" was beginning.

Courtney and Alice took up her cry and followed right on her heels onto the stage with their arms flailing above their heads. "Help us! Help!"

The three girls bolted across the stage and kept going. The audience gasped when they heard three splashes, followed by churning water as the Bunheads waded onto the shore and kept on running.

The gang was too terrified to move. A large figure with a horn sticking out of its head stepped into the half-light and stood dripping before them. Suddenly the monster removed its head.

"I think I'm going to faint," Gwen moaned.

"That darn horse!" Marge Ledbetter growled. "He stepped on my flipper and wouldn't get off it." She shook out her mask and snorkel and set them on the wooden floor. "I was stuck in the mud."

"That was Jingles?" McGee choked out. Suddenly the girls burst into laughter.

"What's so funny?" Marge Ledbetter asked, as she felt her foot to see if it was bruised.

No one could answer. They were laughing too hard. Finally, Rocky managed to answer. "The Bunheads. We were going to get them. But it looks like they just got themselves."

Chapter Fifteen

The final day of camp was a sad one. That morning Mary Bubnik walked around the tent, touching everything and saying, "Good-bye, bed. Good-bye, pillow. Good-bye, rug. Good-bye, tent."

Gwen and McGee's mothers had driven up that morning in Mrs. Hays' big white Cadillac. The ladies met Ron Pulzini and the counselors and heard the story of how Camp Claude Harper creamed Camp Scotsvale in the talent contest.

"You should be very proud of your daughters," Ron Pulzini said. "Their flamenco number was the highlight of the evening."

"Flamenco?" Mrs. Hays looked startled. "But I thought they were here to study ballet."

"We've found that working in another style of

dance can really improve the girls' ballet skills," Miss Gretzky said quickly.

"Really?"

Ron Pulzini looked at Miss Gretzky and then smiled. "Really."

As the day came to an end, most of the girls gathered in the parking lot for a final farewell.

Arvid stood with Rocky by the old blue pickup, surrounded by five different instrument cases.

"Remember," she said, "the first one who learns to swim has to call the other one."

"That's long distance," Rocky said, looping her own bag over her shoulder.

"So call me collect," Arvid replied with the wave of her hand. "My grandparents will love it that I made a friend."

The Rand Band stood on the porch of the lodge playing their instruments, while Miss Gretzky and Marge Ledbetter handed out address lists and hugged each and every girl.

Zan rushed up to Harry Hackerman and pressed a piece of paper into his hand. "Don't read it now," she begged. "It's a poem I wrote about the lake."

"I'm sure it's a good one, coming from the best writer I've ever had." He smiled and tucked it carefully into his shirt pocket. "I'll treasure it."

Mrs. McGee leaned her head out the car window. "I don't want to rush you, girls, but we've got a long drive back."

"Okay, Mom," McGee called. "We'll be right

there." She hurried over to Jingles, who was lazily scratching his back against the tool shed. "Goodbye, boy." She buried her head against the horse's neck. "I'm really going to miss you." She looked up and saw Teague McBride standing with his thumbs looped in his belt. McGee held out her hand. "Thanks for everything."

"Aw, it was nothing," Teague said, shaking her hand. Then he turned to Jingles and added, "Was it?"

The horse tossed his head in a cheerful snort and they both laughed.

Finally, the girls piled into the back seat of the car.

"Where's Gwen?" Mrs. Hays asked, turning around in the seat.

"She's still in our tent," Zan said. "She said she wanted to be alone for a minute."

Gwen sat on the bare mattress of her bed. All the sheets and blankets had been taken back to the main lodge by now. The rug had been rolled up and the place looked very empty. She sighed wistfully and then opened her journal for one final entry.

Dear Diary,

I can't believe my luck. Birch Patrol finally got to eat first and what did they serve us? Eggs Surprise. For your information, that's eggs on a tortilla covered in something green and slimy. Gag me with a canoe!

After breakfast we sang "Auld Lang Syne" and everybody cried. Ol' Leadbottom was blubbering the loudest. Miss Gretzky made the announcement that she would be taking ballet lessons, and then Teague told us he was quitting Camp Scotsvale.

There are a lot of things I'm not going to miss about this place — the outhouses, the bugs, and the food. But there are many more things I will miss — J.P., and Arvid, and the Rand Band. And, of course, all of the counselors. And this may sound weird, but I think I'm going to miss Ol' Leadbottom most of all.

Your friend,
Gwen

Gwen paused to rub her eyes. She fought hard to swallow the lump that was forming in her throat. Finally she looked back down at the page.

P.S. See you next year!

136

Bad News Ballet

Coming soon:
#9 Boo Who?

"Come on," Zan said, slipping her purple beret on her head and pulling on her trench coat.

"But what about ballet rehearsal?" Mary Bubnik asked. "We're supposed to be at the auditorium in fifteen minutes."

"We want to be at the scene of the crime first, though, to look for clues," Zan answered.

"Clues?" Rocky paused with one arm through the sleeve of her red satin jacket with her name embroidered in silver letters across the back.

"Uh oh," Gwen muttered. "Zan's got that Tiffany Truenote, Teen Detective look in her eye."

"What's that mean?" Mary Bubnik asked, as she zipped up her pink parka.

McGee tossed her scarf over her shoulder. "It means we're going hunting for the Monster of Mulberry Avenue."

Get ready for fun
because you're invited to the...

Bad News Ballet

by Jahnna N. Malcolm

Ballet is *bad news* for McGee, Gwen, Mary Bubnik, Zan, and Rocky! Zan would rather be reading a good book, Mary Bubnik is a dancing klutz, Gwen prefers Twinkies to *pliés*, McGee's busy with her hockey team, and Rocky is just too cool for leotards and pink tights. Who would ever think they'd be ballerinas...or the best of friends!

It's the funniest performance ever!

❏ ME41915-3	#1	**The Terrible Tryouts**	**$2.50**
❏ ME41916-1	#2	**Battle of the Bunheads**	**$2.50**
❏ ME42474-2	#3	**Stupid Cupids**	**$2.75**
❏ ME42472-6	#4	**Who Framed Mary Bubnik?**	**$2.75**
❏ ME42888-8	#5	**Blubberina**	**$2.75**
❏ ME42889-6	#6	**Save D.A.D.!**	**$2.75**
❏ ME43395-4	#7	**The King and Us**	**$2.75**
❏ ME43396-2	#8	**Camp Clodhopper**	**$2.75**

Watch for new titles coming soon!
Available wherever you buy books, or use coupon below.